NADJA SPIEGELMAN & SERGIO GARCÍ

BLANCAFLOR

THE HERO WITH
SECRET POWERS

A FOLKTALE FROM LATIN AMERICA

A TOON GRAPHIC
TOON BOOKS, NEW YORK

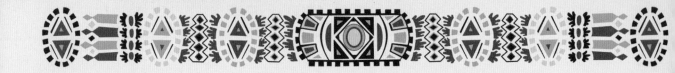

UPDATED FAIRY TALES FO

by F. Isabel Campoy

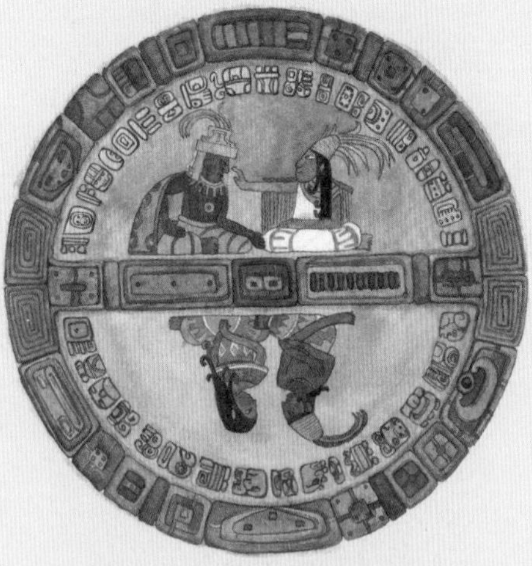

In Blanca Flor, Una princesa maya, *(illustration above by Rafael Yockteng,) the author, Victor Montejo, tells the story of Blancaflor as he heard it from his grandmother while growing up in Maya Jacaltec culture. The heroine is a Maya princess and her father, W'itz Ak'al, is a demigod, the Lord of the Forest.*

Why do we keep turning to folk and fairy tales from long ago? What can we get from reading about ogres and magic spells that is relevant to us today, to our lives in the age of the Internet? These tales have the power to open up our imagination. They resonate within our truest selves, the part of us that discovered the world when we were children and forms the core of who we are. A story like *Blancaflor*, which appears in many versions throughout Latin America, gives us a safe place to experience delight and terror in rapid turns while offering the promise of a happy ending. Folktales, passed down orally through generations, also show us the world by teaching us the customs, values, and cultural traditions of a people. Fairy tales may be populated by giants and talking stones, but they also take us into the homes of common folk solving real-life problems.

The Latin American heritage is richly diverse, a unique blend of Old World and New, spanning a continent across many geographic boundaries and cultures. When the Spaniards landed in the 15th century, they brought their medieval stories brimming with princesses and dragons. But since Spain is itself a land at the crossroads of many

TELL YOUR OWN STORY

It is part of the oral tradition for the performer to embroider the tale and make it his or her own. Storytellers like to use stock phrases to capture their audience's attention when they start and end their stories. Here are some of them, in Spanish and English:

¿Quieres que te cuente un cuento?
Do you want to hear a story?

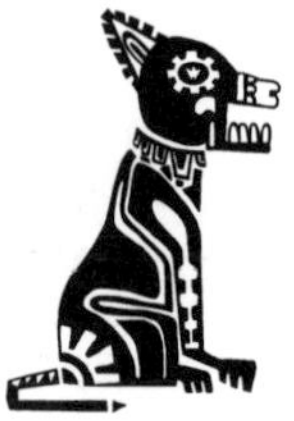

Había una vez.../ Érase una vez...
Once upon a time...

Hace mucho tiempo...
A long time ago...

Cuentan que...
The story goes that...

En un país muy lejano...
In a far-off land...

En la tierra del olvido, donde de nada nadie se acuerda, había...
In the land where all is forgotten, where no one remembers anything, there was...

...y colorín colorado, este cuento se ha acabado.
...and so, my fine-feathered friend,
now the story has found an end.

...y vivieron felices para siempre.
...and everyone lived happily ever after.

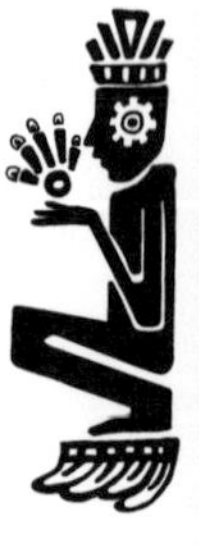

From *Tales Our Abuelitas Told*,
by F. Isabel Campoy and Alma Flor Ada

THE 21ST CENTURY

cultures, these tales already contained Catholic, Jewish, Arab, and Moorish influences. The Europeans' encounter with Maya, Aztec, Inca, and other Native American cultures—themselves spread widely across land and time—produced one of the world's most diverse and varied storytelling traditions. Everything that happens in the land of the popular *cuentos*, or fairy tales, was once invented by the pure magic of a storyteller's fertile imagination. As the stories grew and changed with every telling, the anecdotal became universal. Folktales often contain moral lessons; instead of telling us how to behave, they show us the implications of good and bad behavior. They also help us develop our social and emotional intelligence as we empathize with the different perspectives of the heroes and villains.

Blancaflor was one of the stories included in the 1946 collection, Spanish Fairy Stories, translated by Gary Woolsey. In the illustration by Mario Hubert Armengold above, the prince travels on a winged horse.

WITHDRAWN

A recurring theme in the Latino experience is a celebration of strong women. Like so many *señoras* and *señoritas* in Hispanic families, the independent mothers, sisters, and daughters in these folktales have the inner strength to rise above obstacles and to overcome adversity. But above all, the reality of Latin American folktales is that, as in Blancaflor's story, magic is in all of us. Listen to this story and tell it to others: you, too, may discover that you have a secret power, the power of storytelling.

F. ISABEL CAMPOY and **ALMA FLOR ADA** are authors of many award-winning children's books, including *Tales Our Abuelitas Told*, a collection of Hispanic folktales that includes their version of BLANCAFLOR. As scholars devoted to the study of language and literacy, Alma Flor and Isabel love to share Hispanic and Latino culture with young readers. "Folktales are a valuable heritage we have received from the past, and we must treasure them and pass them along," Isabel says. "If you do not have roots, you will not have fruits."

Also by the same authors:
LOST IN NYC: A SUBWAY ADVENTURE
recipient of six starred reviews and many awards and distinctions, including a School Library Journal's Best Book of the Year and an American Library Association's Notable Children's Book

For Françoise –NS
For Alicia and Pablo –SGS & LM

A JUNIOR LIBRARY
GUILD SELECTION

Editorial Direction and Book Design: FRANÇOISE MOULY

Research Associate: MARÍA E. SANTANA

Endpapers, Aztec Designs and Motifs: GENEVIEVE BORMES

Colors: LOLA MORAL

SERGIO GARCÍA SÁNCHEZ'S & LOLA MORAL'S artwork was drawn and colored digitally

FOR VISUAL READERS
TOON
GRAPHICS

A TOON Graphic™ © 2021 Nadja Spiegelman, Sergio García Sánchez & TOON Books, an imprint of RAW Junior, LLC, 27 Greene Street, New York, NY 10013. TOON Books® and TOON Graphics™ are trademarks of RAW Junior, LLC. All rights reserved. No part of this book may be used or reproduced in any manner whatsoever without written permission except in the case of brief quotations embodied in critical articles and reviews. Library of Congress Cataloging-in-Publication Data: Names: Spiegelman, Nadja, author. | García Sánchez, Sergio, 1967- illustrator. Title: Blancaflor, the hero with secret powers : a folktale from Latin America / Nadja Spiegelman & Sergio García Sánchez. Description: New York : TOON Books, 2021- | Includes bibliographical references. | Summary: "In this updated adaptation of a classic Latin American folktale, Blancaflor, a young ogre with magical powers, decides to secretly help a charming prince who has made a foolish bet with her father. Through saving the prince and the kingdom, she learns to be honest with herself and others about the things that make her special"-- Provided by publisher. Identifiers: LCCN 2021007309 Subjects: LCSH: Graphic novels. | CYAC: Graphic novels. | Fairy tales. | Ghouls and ogres--Fiction. | Princes--Fiction. | Magic--Fiction. | Ability--Fiction. | Fantasy. Classification: LCC PZ7.7.S65 Bla 2021 | DDC 741.5/973--dc23 LC record available at https://lccn.loc.gov/2021007309 All our books are Smyth Sewn (the highest library-quality binding available) and printed with soy-based inks on acid-free, woodfree paper harvested from responsible sources. Printed in China by C&C Offset Printing Co., Ltd. Distributed to the trade by Consortium Book Sales & Distribution, a division of Ingram Content Group; orders (866) 400-5351; ips@ingramcontent.com; www.cbsd.com. A Spanish edition, *BLANCAFLOR, la heroína con poderes secretos: un cuento de Latinoamérica*, is also available.

ISBN 978-1-943145-55-3 (hardcover English edition)
ISBN 978-1-943145-56-0 (softcover English edition)
ISBN 978-1-943145-57-7 (hardcover Spanish edition)
ISBN 978-1-943145-58-4 (softcover Spanish edition)
21 22 23 24 25 26 C&C 10 9 8 7 6 5 4 3 2 1
www.TOON-BOOKS.com

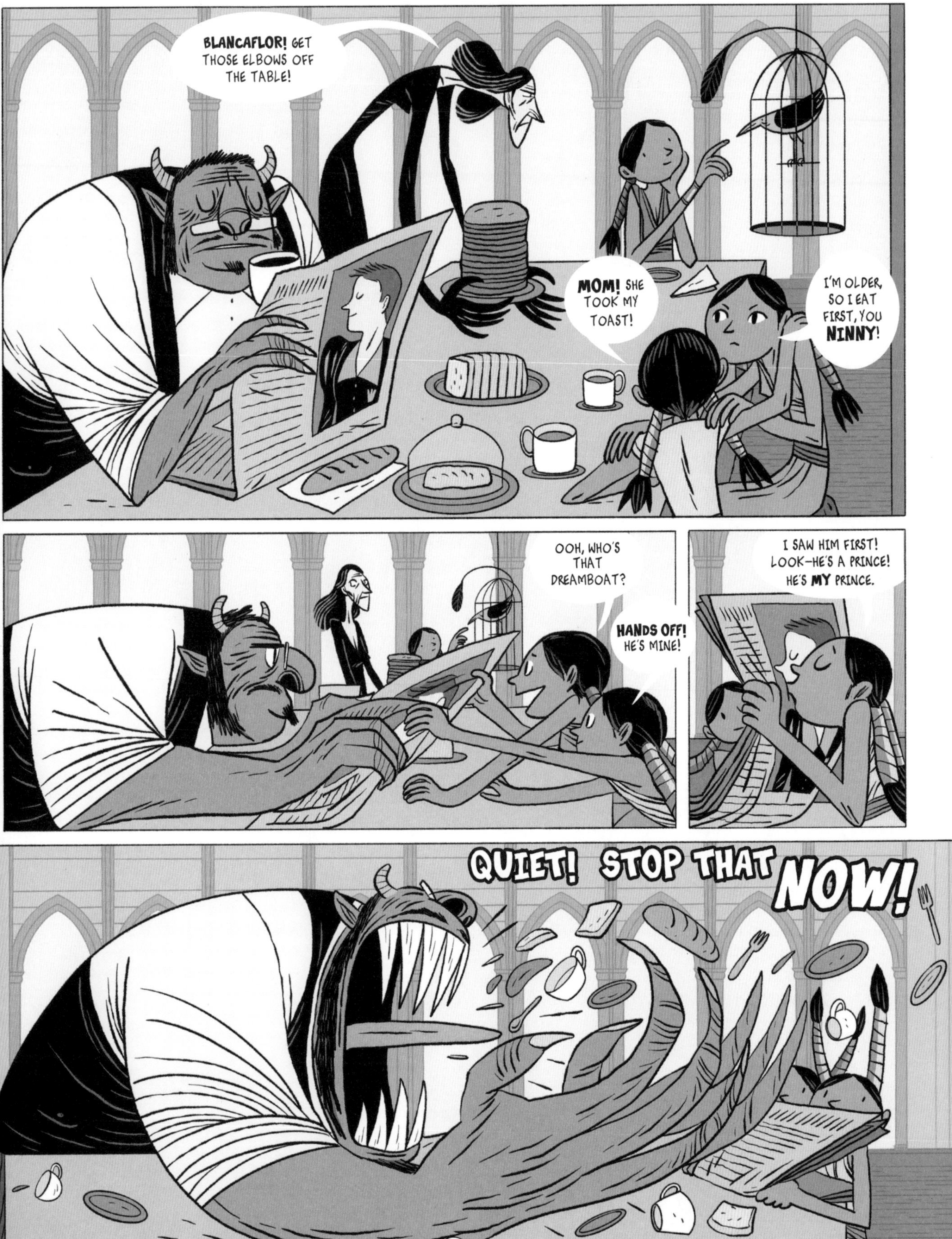

BLANCAFLOR! GET THOSE ELBOWS OFF THE TABLE!
MOM! SHE TOOK MY TOAST!
I'M OLDER, SO I EAT FIRST, YOU NINNY!
OOH, WHO'S THAT DREAMBOAT?
HANDS OFF! HE'S MINE!
I SAW HIM FIRST! LOOK—HE'S A PRINCE! HE'S MY PRINCE.
QUIET! STOP THAT NOW!

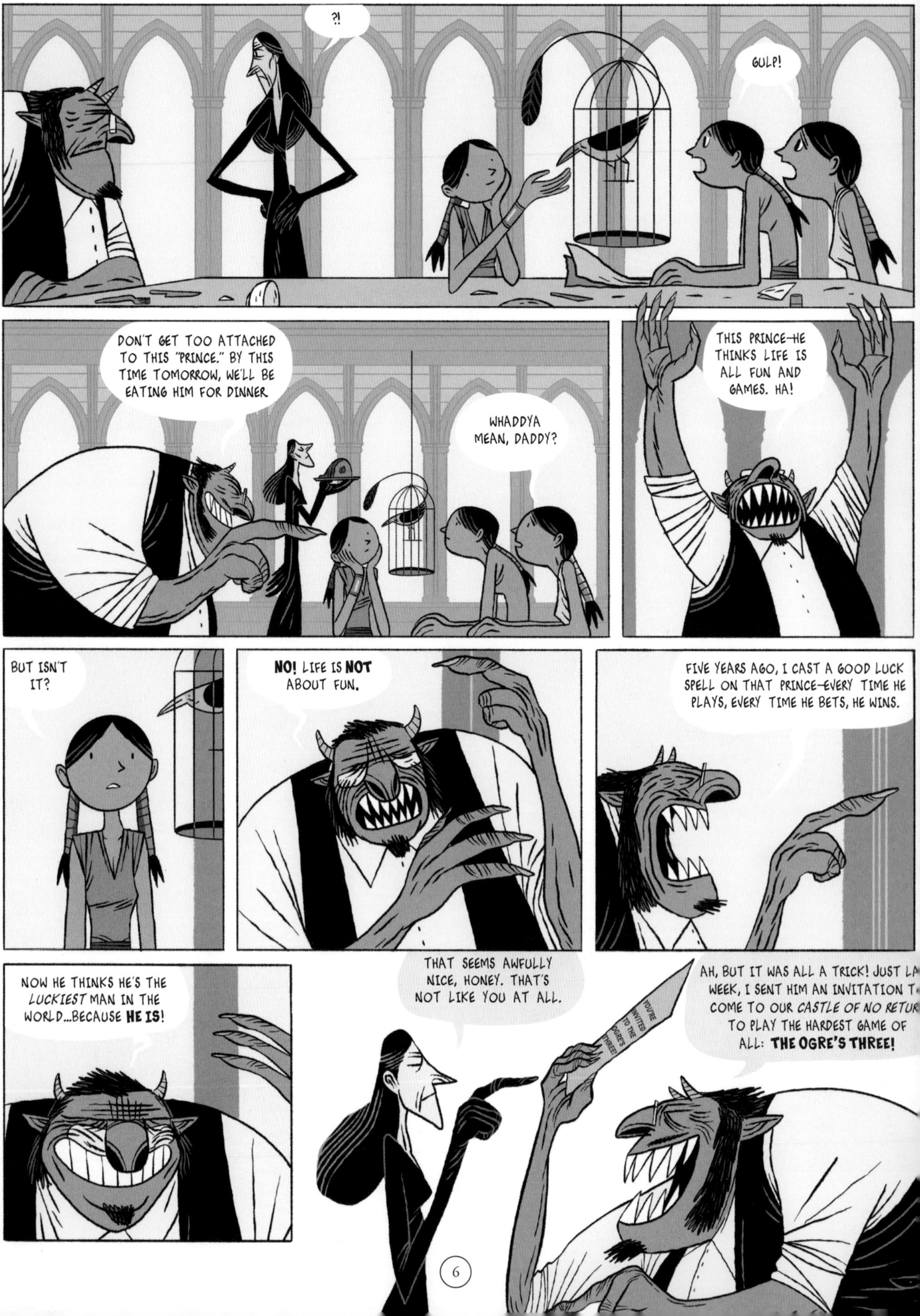
?!
GULP!
DON'T GET TOO ATTACHED TO THIS "PRINCE." BY THIS TIME TOMORROW, WE'LL BE EATING HIM FOR DINNER
WHADDYA MEAN, DADDY?
THIS PRINCE—HE THINKS LIFE IS ALL FUN AND GAMES. HA!
BUT ISN'T IT?
NO! LIFE IS **NOT** ABOUT FUN.
FIVE YEARS AGO, I CAST A GOOD LUCK SPELL ON THAT PRINCE—EVERY TIME HE PLAYS, EVERY TIME HE BETS, HE WINS.
NOW HE THINKS HE'S THE *LUCKIEST* MAN IN THE WORLD...BECAUSE **HE IS**!
THAT SEEMS AWFULLY NICE, HONEY. THAT'S NOT LIKE YOU AT ALL.
YOU'RE INVITED TO THE OGRE'S THREE!
AH, BUT IT WAS ALL A TRICK! JUST LA
WEEK, I SENT HIM AN INVITATION T
COME TO OUR *CASTLE OF NO RETUR*
TO PLAY THE HARDEST GAME OF ALL: **THE OGRE'S THREE!**

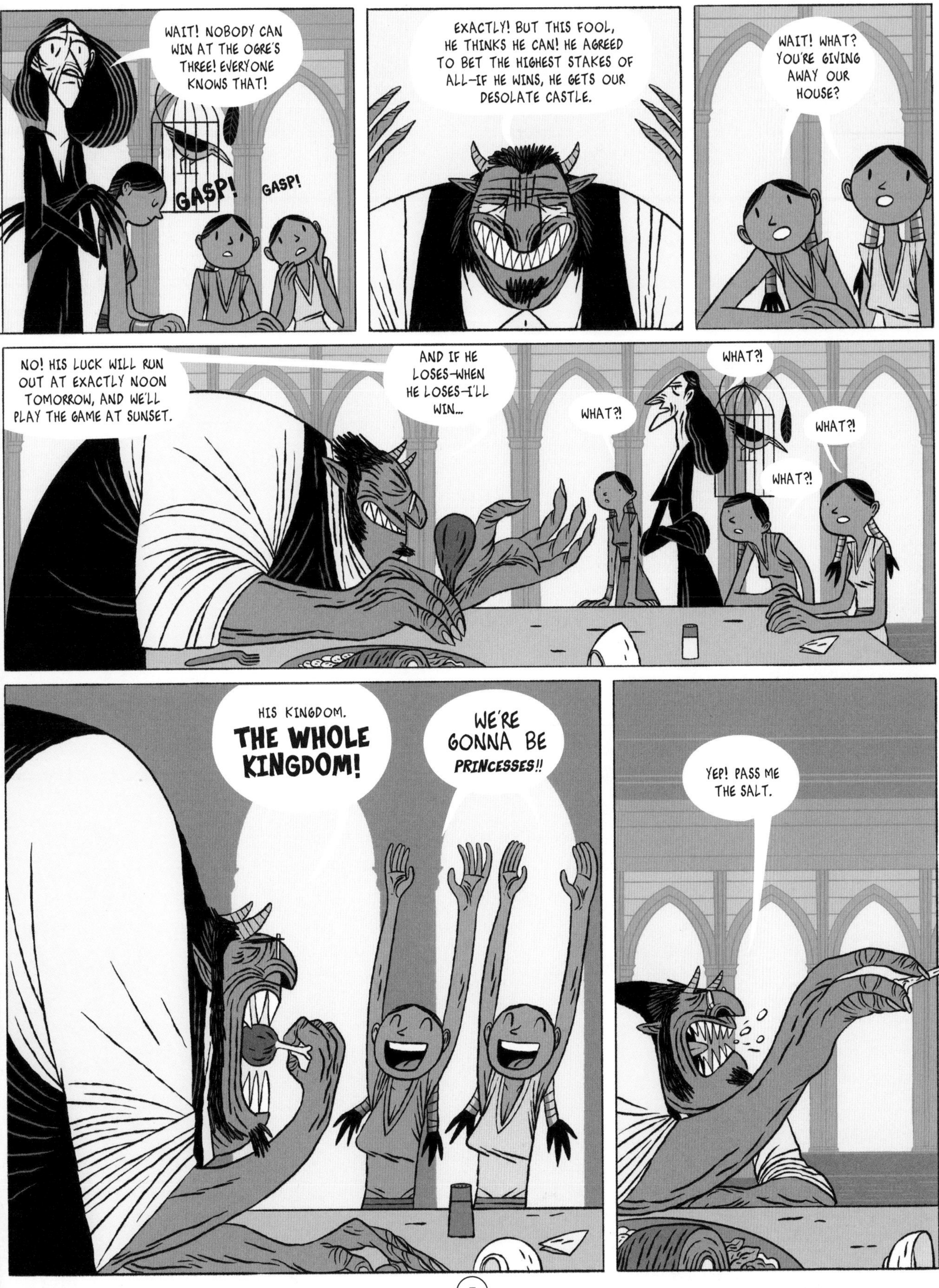
WAIT! NOBODY CAN WIN AT THE OGRE'S THREE! EVERYONE KNOWS THAT!
GASP!
GASP!
EXACTLY! BUT THIS FOOL, HE THINKS HE CAN! HE AGREED TO BET THE HIGHEST STAKES OF ALL—IF HE WINS, HE GETS OUR DESOLATE CASTLE.
WAIT! WHAT? YOU'RE GIVING AWAY OUR HOUSE?
NO! HIS LUCK WILL RUN OUT AT EXACTLY NOON TOMORROW, AND WE'LL PLAY THE GAME AT SUNSET.
AND IF HE LOSES—WHEN HE LOSES—I'LL WIN...
WHAT?!
WHAT?!
WHAT?!
WHAT?!
HIS KINGDOM. THE WHOLE KINGDOM!
WE'RE GONNA BE PRINCESSES!!
YEP! PASS ME THE SALT.

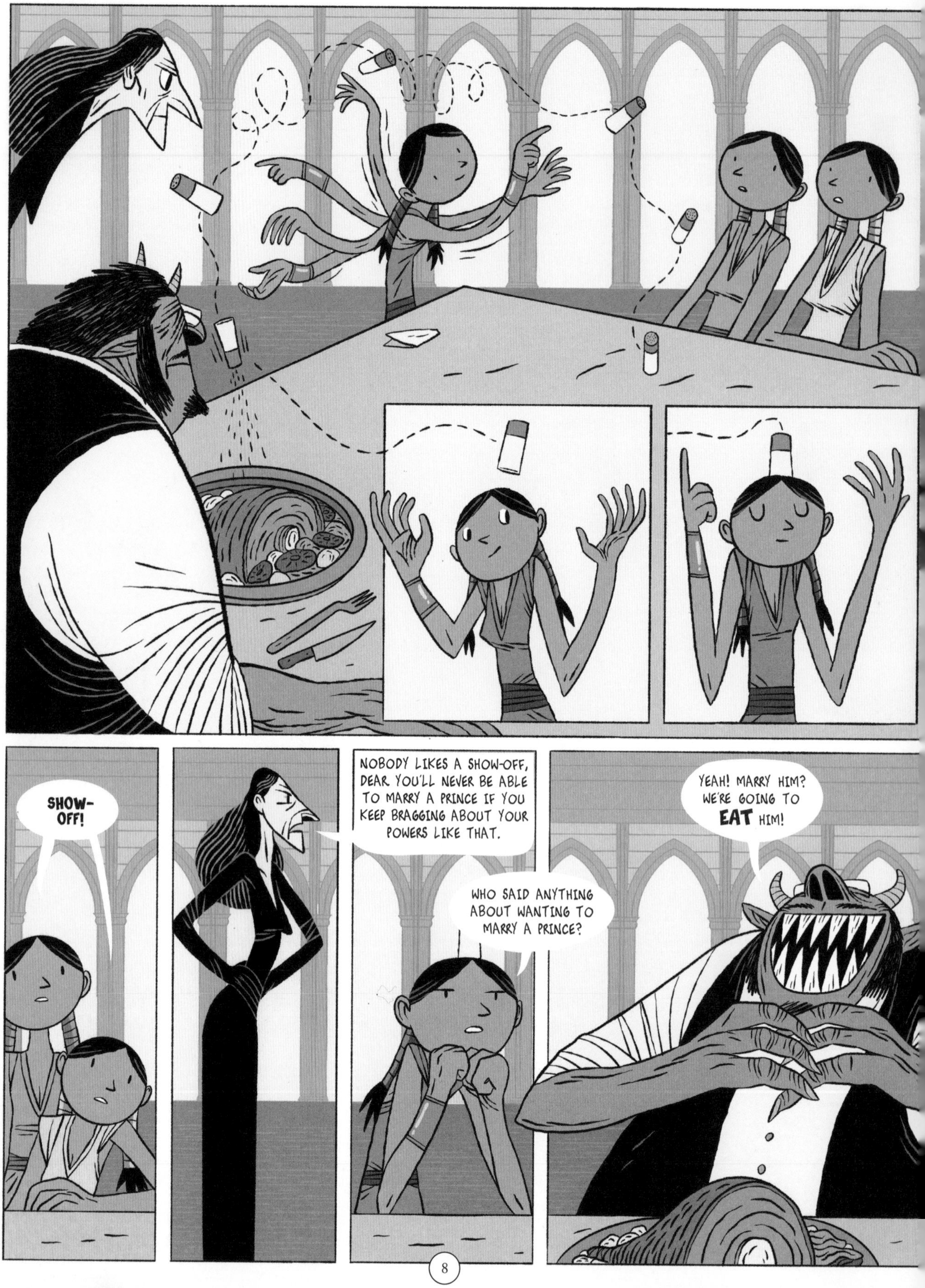
SHOW-OFF!
NOBODY LIKES A SHOW-OFF, DEAR YOU'LL NEVER BE ABLE TO MARRY A PRINCE IF YOU KEEP BRAGGING ABOUT YOUR POWERS LIKE THAT.
WHO SAID ANYTHING ABOUT WANTING TO MARRY A PRINCE?
YEAH! MARRY HIM? WE'RE GOING TO EAT HIM!

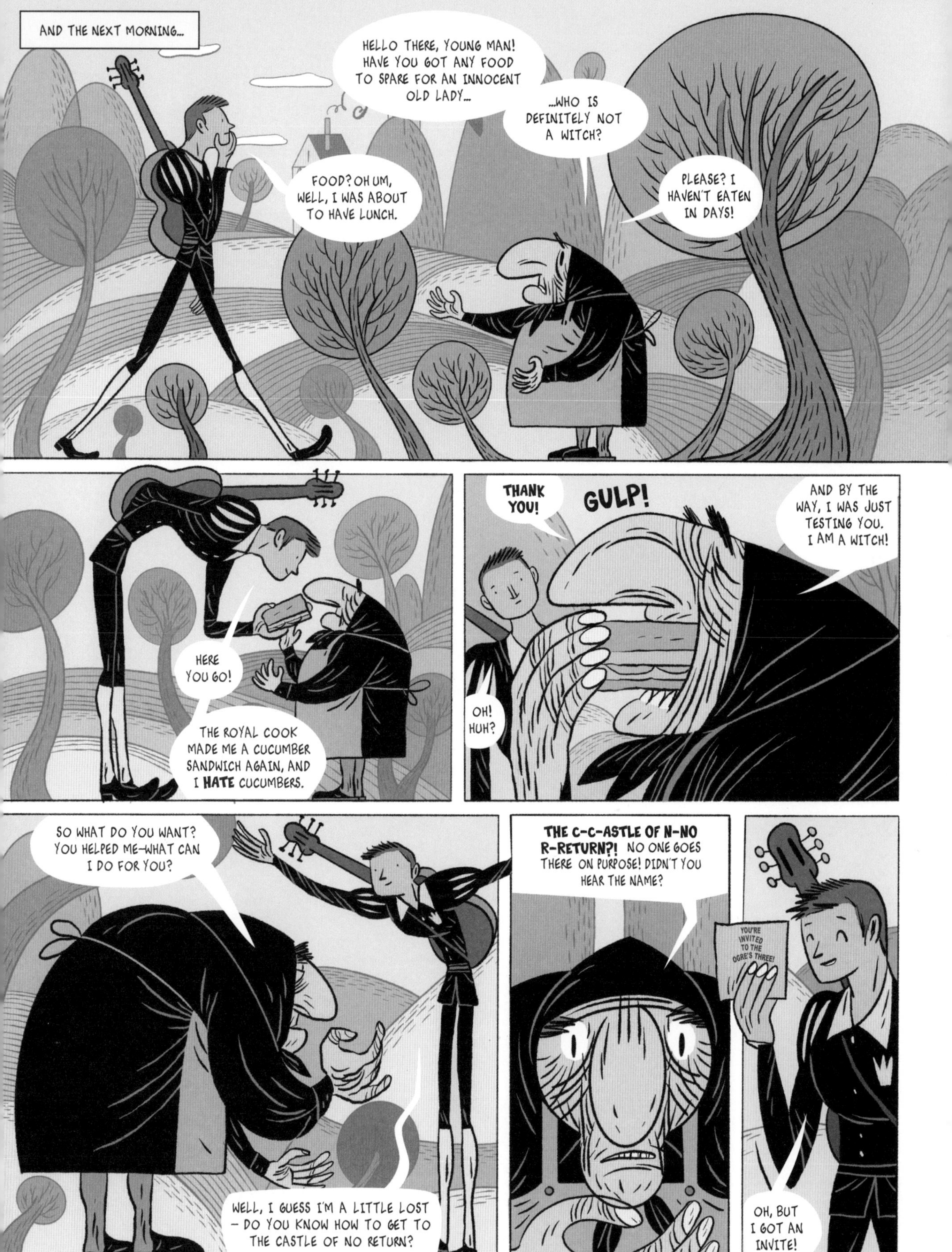
AND THE NEXT MORNING...
HELLO THERE, YOUNG MAN! HAVE YOU GOT ANY FOOD TO SPARE FOR AN INNOCENT OLD LADY...
...WHO IS DEFINITELY NOT A WITCH?
FOOD? OH UM, WELL, I WAS ABOUT TO HAVE LUNCH.
PLEASE? I HAVEN'T EATEN IN DAYS!
HERE YOU GO!
THE ROYAL COOK MADE ME A CUCUMBER SANDWICH AGAIN, AND I **HATE** CUCUMBERS.
THANK YOU!
GULP!
AND BY THE WAY, I WAS JUST TESTING YOU. I AM A WITCH!
OH! HUH?
SO WHAT DO YOU WANT? YOU HELPED ME—WHAT CAN I DO FOR YOU?
WELL, I GUESS I'M A LITTLE LOST - DO YOU KNOW HOW TO GET TO THE CASTLE OF NO RETURN?
THE C-C-ASTLE OF N-NO R-RETURN?! NO ONE GOES THERE ON PURPOSE! DIDN'T YOU HEAR THE NAME?
YOU'RE INVITED TO THE OGRE'S THREE!
OH, BUT I GOT AN INVITE!

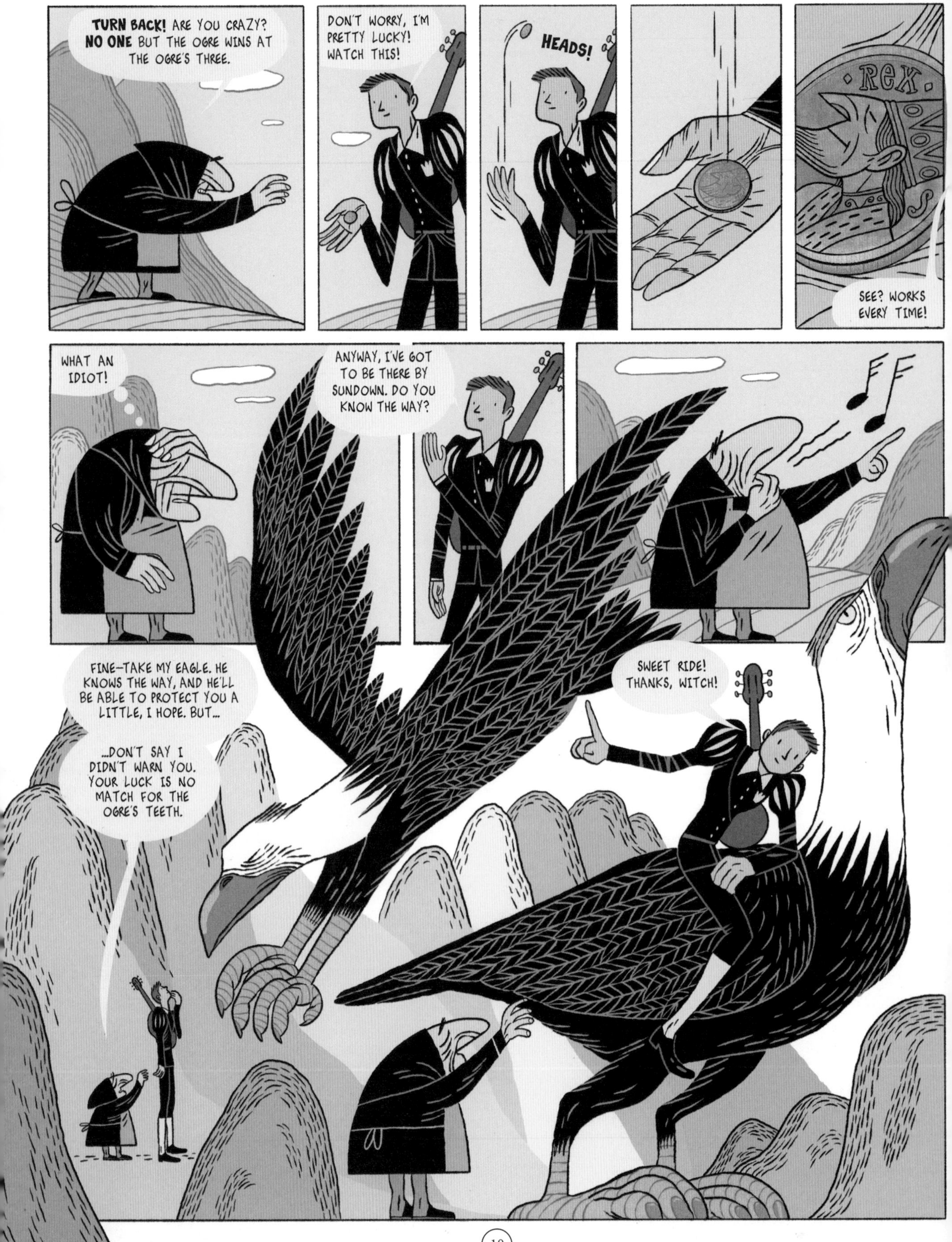
TURN BACK! ARE YOU CRAZY? NO ONE BUT THE OGRE WINS AT THE OGRE'S THREE.
DON'T WORRY, I'M PRETTY LUCKY! WATCH THIS!
HEADS!
REX
SEE? WORKS EVERY TIME!
WHAT AN IDIOT!
ANYWAY, I'VE GOT TO BE THERE BY SUNDOWN. DO YOU KNOW THE WAY?
FINE—TAKE MY EAGLE. HE KNOWS THE WAY, AND HE'LL BE ABLE TO PROTECT YOU A LITTLE, I HOPE. BUT...
...DON'T SAY I DIDN'T WARN YOU. YOUR LUCK IS NO MATCH FOR THE OGRE'S TEETH.
SWEET RIDE! THANKS, WITCH!

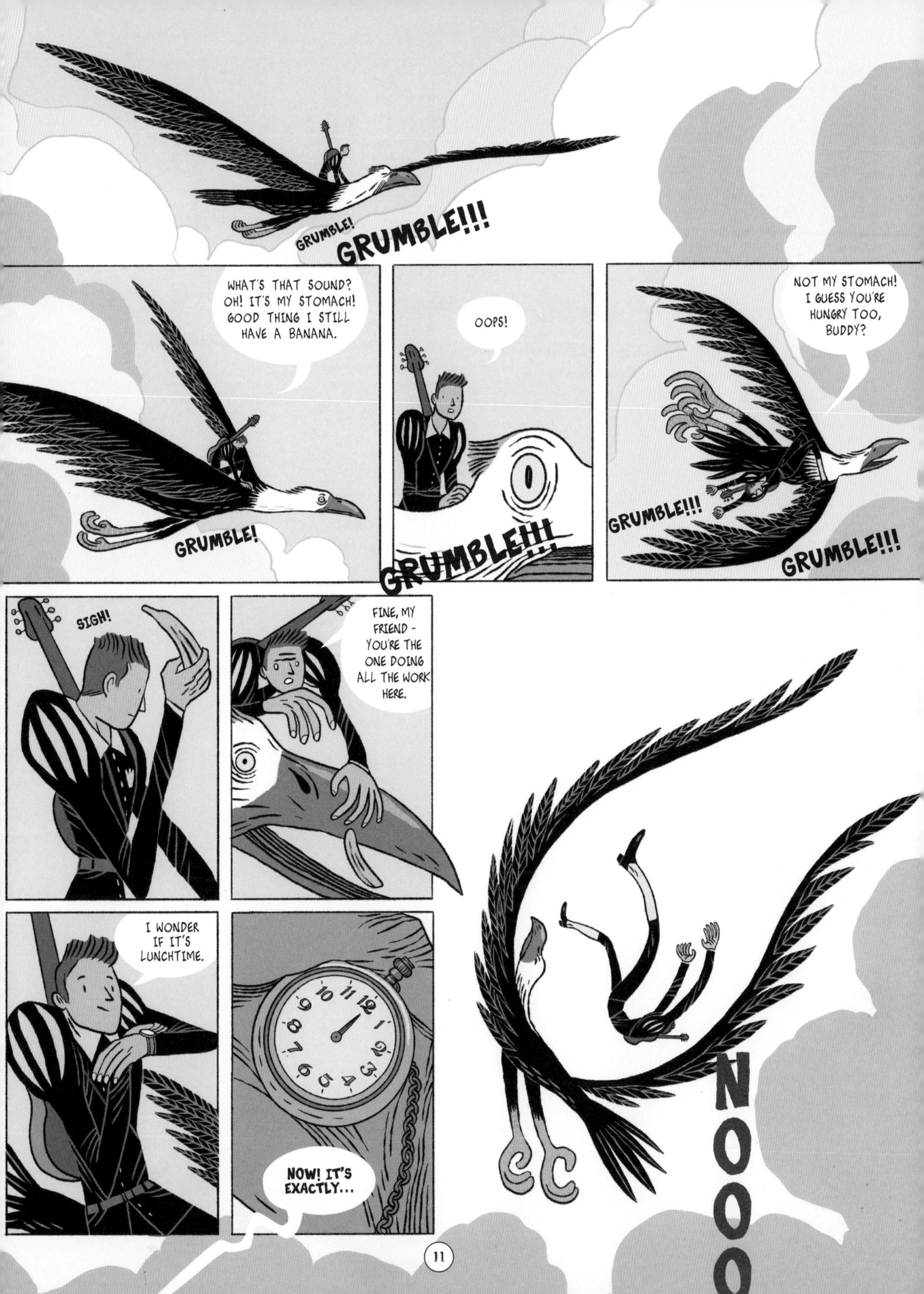
GRUMBLE!
GRUMBLE!!!
WHAT'S THAT SOUND? OH! IT'S MY STOMACH! GOOD THING I STILL HAVE A BANANA.
GRUMBLE!
OOPS!
GRUMBLE!!!
NOT MY STOMACH! I GUESS YOU'RE HUNGRY TOO, BUDDY?
GRUMBLE!!!
GRUMBLE!!!
SIGH!
FINE, MY FRIEND - YOU'RE THE ONE DOING ALL THE WORK HERE.
I WONDER IF IT'S LUNCHTIME.
NOW! IT'S EXACTLY...
NOOO

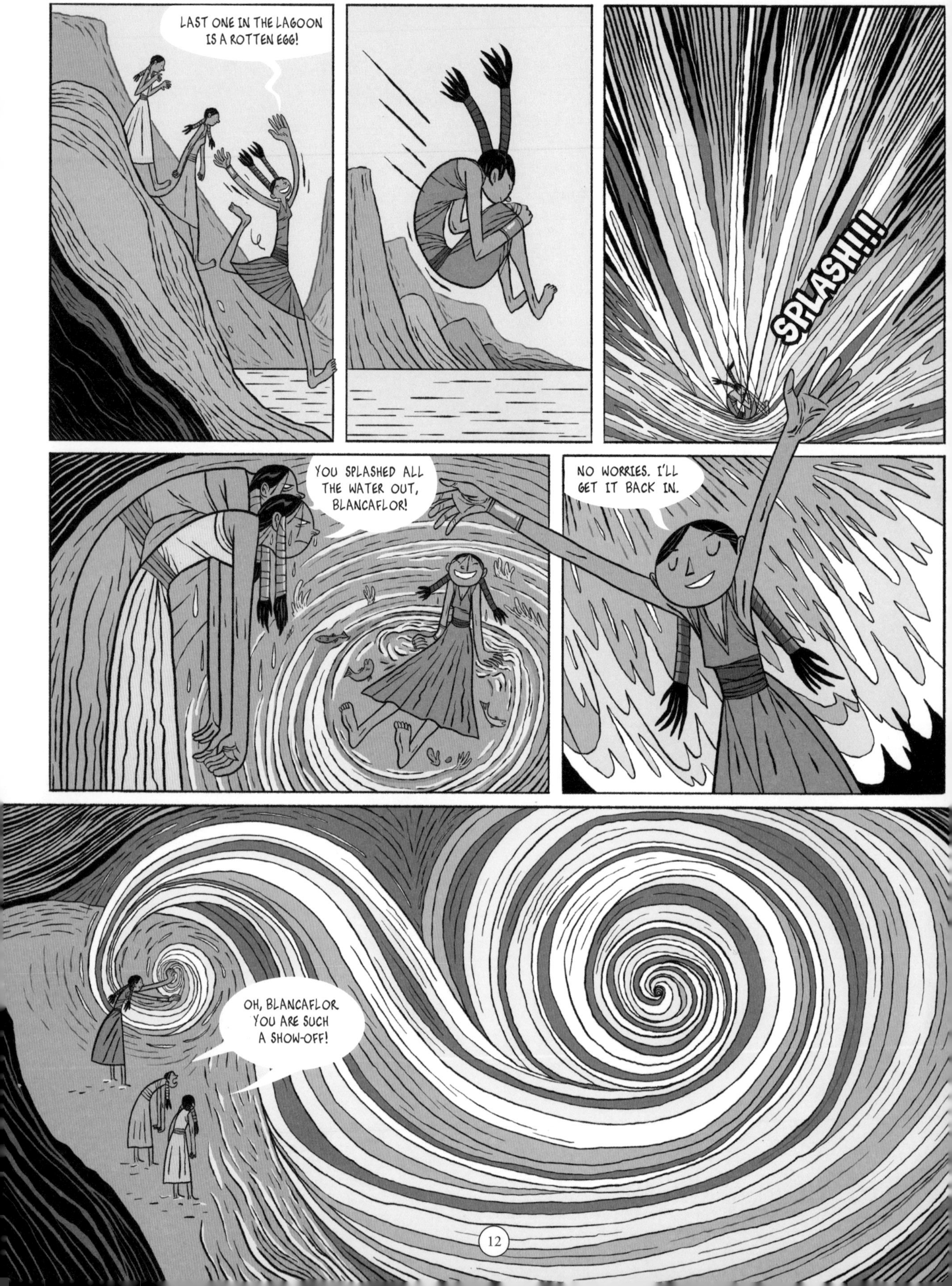

LAST ONE IN THE LAGOON IS A ROTTEN EGG!
SPLASH!!!!
YOU SPLASHED ALL THE WATER OUT, BLANCAFLOR!
NO WORRIES. I'LL GET IT BACK IN.
OH, BLANCAFLOR YOU ARE SUCH A SHOW-OFF!

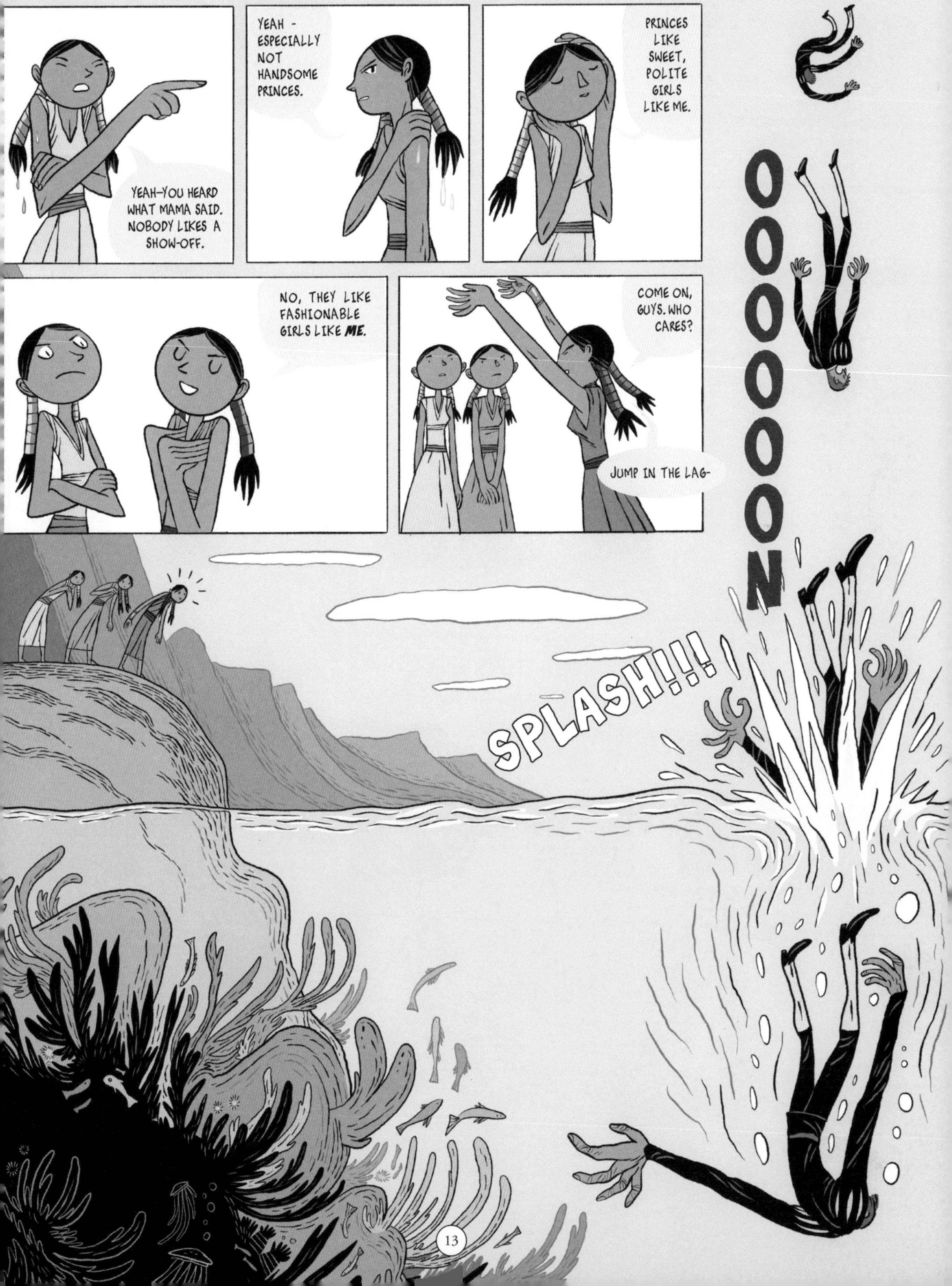
YEAH—YOU HEARD WHAT MAMA SAID. NOBODY LIKES A SHOW-OFF.
YEAH - ESPECIALLY NOT HANDSOME PRINCES.
PRINCES LIKE SWEET, POLITE GIRLS LIKE ME.
NO, THEY LIKE FASHIONABLE GIRLS LIKE **ME**.
COME ON, GUYS. WHO CARES?
JUMP IN THE LAG-
OOOOOOON
SPLASH!!!!

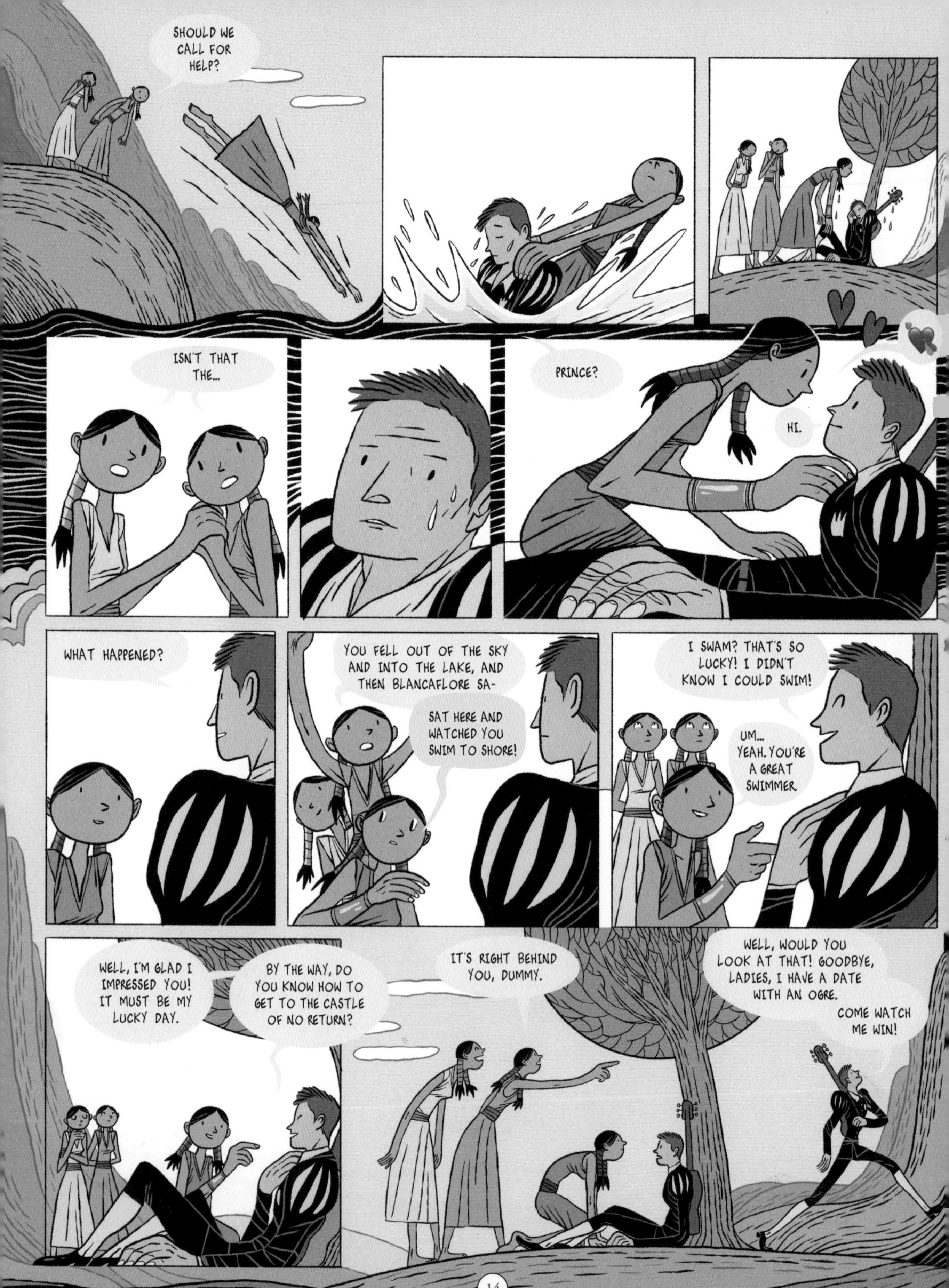
SHOULD WE CALL FOR HELP?
ISN'T THAT THE...
PRINCE?
HI.
WHAT HAPPENED?
YOU FELL OUT OF THE SKY AND INTO THE LAKE, AND THEN BLANCAFLORE SA-
SAT HERE AND WATCHED YOU SWIM TO SHORE!
I SWAM? THAT'S SO LUCKY! I DIDN'T KNOW I COULD SWIM!
UM... YEAH. YOU'RE A GREAT SWIMMER
WELL, I'M GLAD I IMPRESSED YOU! IT MUST BE MY LUCKY DAY.
BY THE WAY, DO YOU KNOW HOW TO GET TO THE CASTLE OF NO RETURN?
IT'S RIGHT BEHIND YOU, DUMMY.
WELL, WOULD YOU LOOK AT THAT! GOODBYE, LADIES, I HAVE A DATE WITH AN OGRE.
COME WATCH ME WIN!

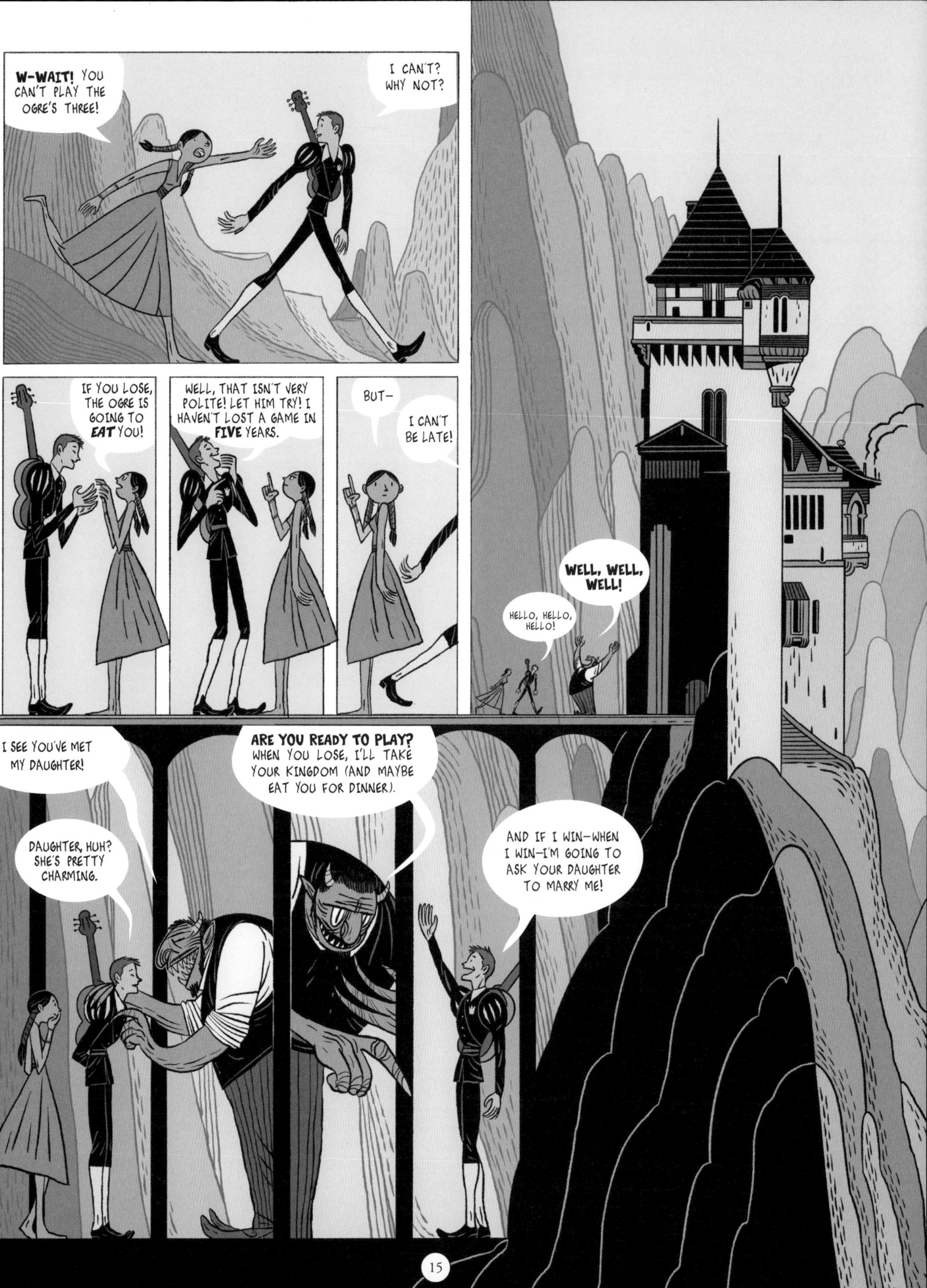

W-WAIT! YOU CAN'T PLAY THE OGRE'S THREE!
I CAN'T? WHY NOT?
IF YOU LOSE, THE OGRE IS GOING TO EAT YOU!
WELL, THAT ISN'T VERY POLITE! LET HIM TRY! I HAVEN'T LOST A GAME IN FIVE YEARS.
BUT–
I CAN'T BE LATE!
WELL, WELL, WELL!
HELLO, HELLO, HELLO!
I SEE YOU'VE MET MY DAUGHTER!
DAUGHTER, HUH? SHE'S PRETTY CHARMING.
ARE YOU READY TO PLAY? WHEN YOU LOSE, I'LL TAKE YOUR KINGDOM (AND MAYBE EAT YOU FOR DINNER).
AND IF I WIN–WHEN I WIN–I'M GOING TO ASK YOUR DAUGHTER TO MARRY ME!

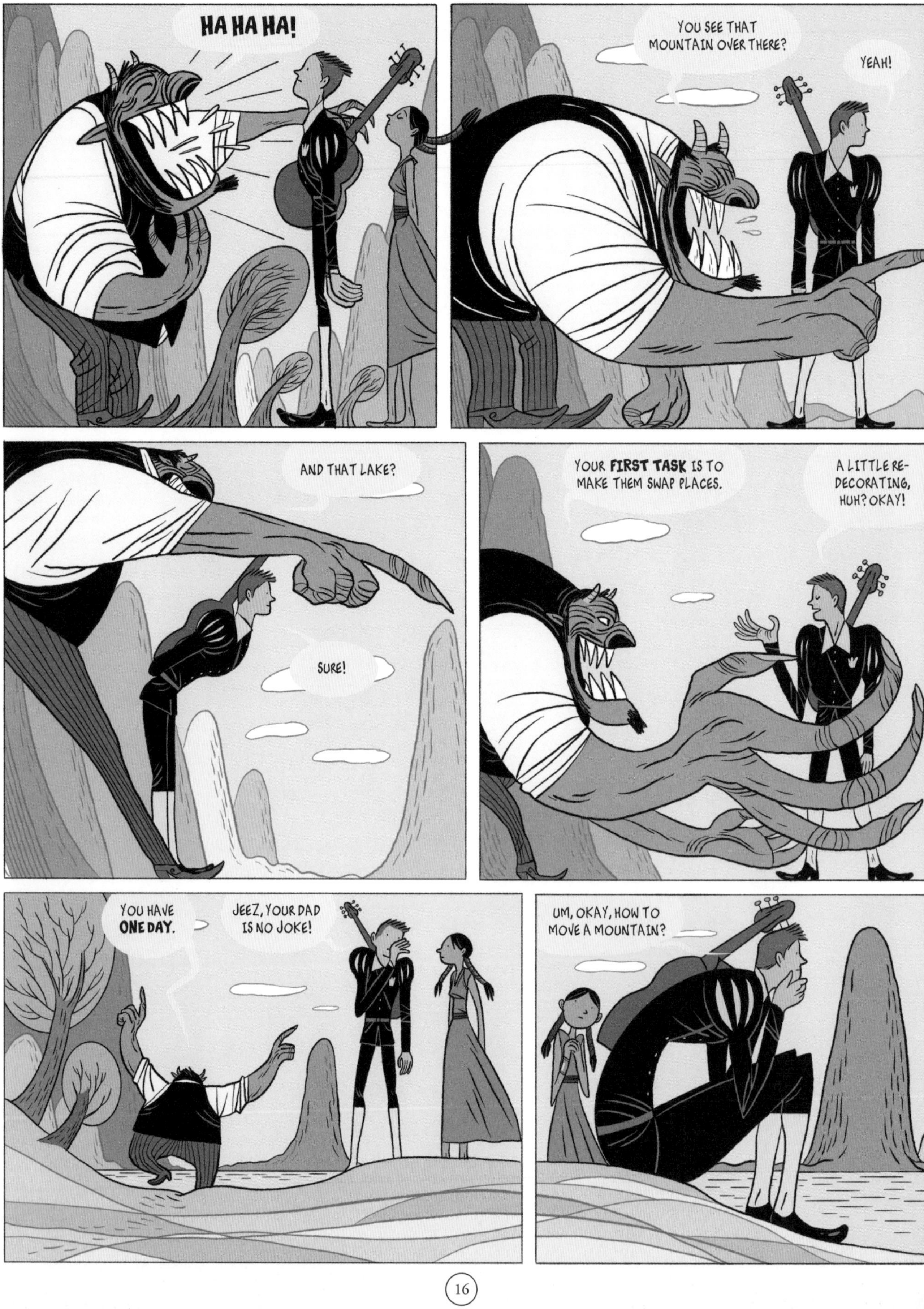
HA HA HA!
YOU SEE THAT MOUNTAIN OVER THERE?
YEAH!
AND THAT LAKE?
SURE!
YOUR FIRST TASK IS TO MAKE THEM SWAP PLACES.
A LITTLE RE-DECORATING, HUH? OKAY!
YOU HAVE ONE DAY.
JEEZ, YOUR DAD IS NO JOKE!
UM, OKAY, HOW TO MOVE A MOUNTAIN?

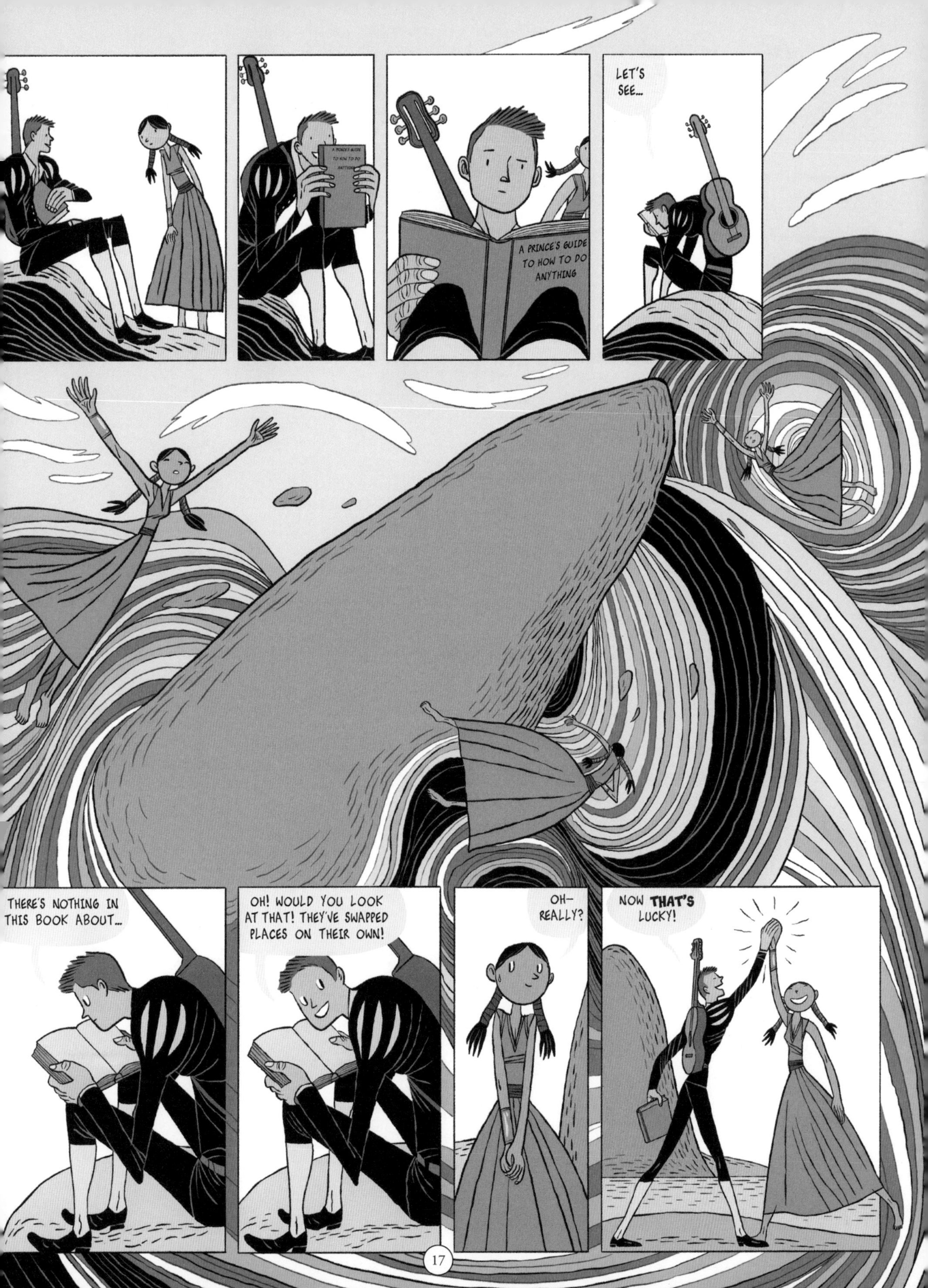
A PRINCE'S GUIDE TO HOW TO DO ANYTHING
LET'S SEE...
THERE'S NOTHING IN THIS BOOK ABOUT...
OH! WOULD YOU LOOK AT THAT! THEY'VE SWAPPED PLACES ON THEIR OWN!
OH– REALLY?
NOW **THAT'S** LUCKY!

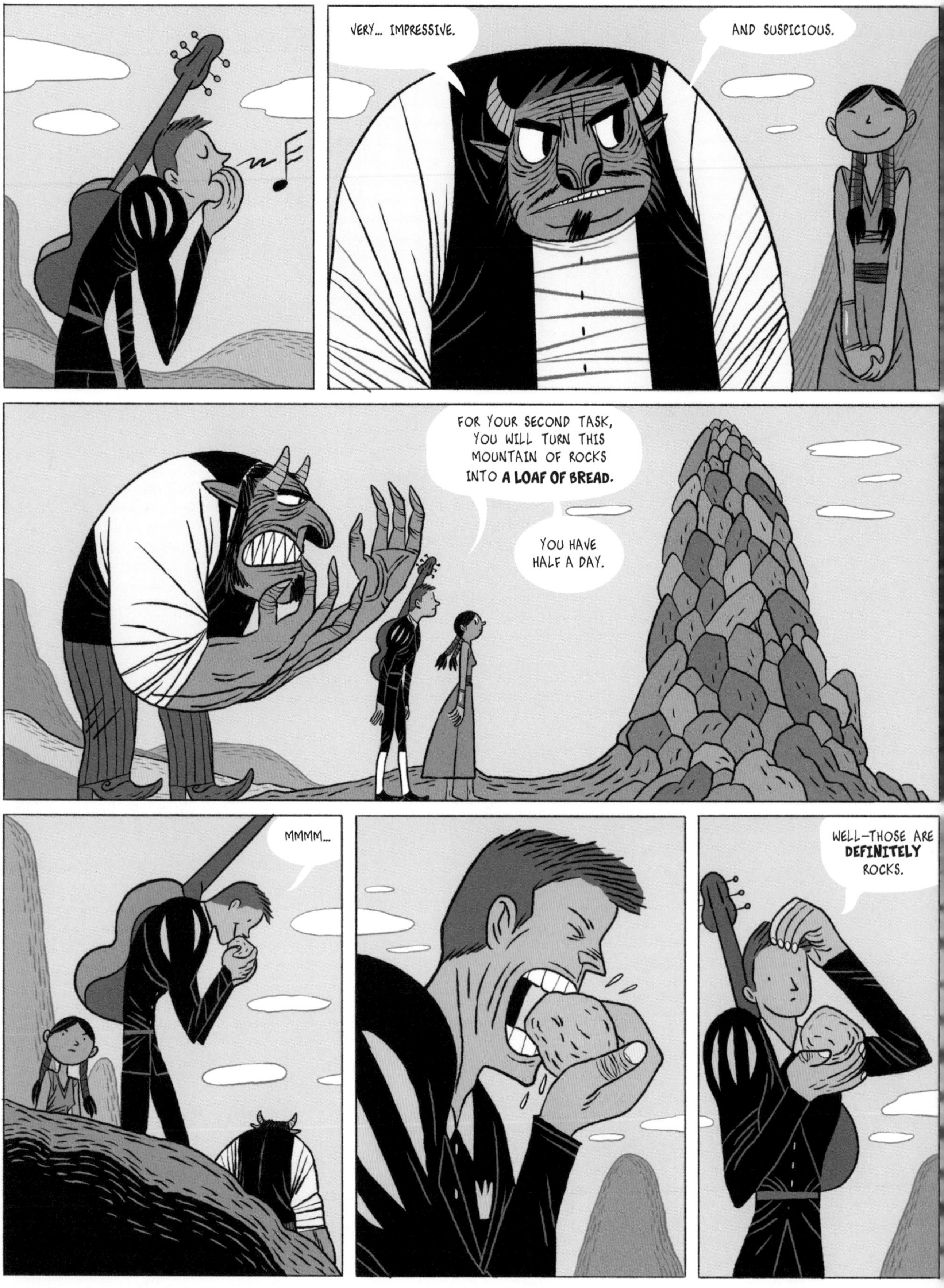
VERY... IMPRESSIVE.
AND SUSPICIOUS.
FOR YOUR SECOND TASK, YOU WILL TURN THIS MOUNTAIN OF ROCKS INTO **A LOAF OF BREAD.**
YOU HAVE HALF A DAY.
MMMM...
WELL–THOSE ARE **DEFINITELY** ROCKS.

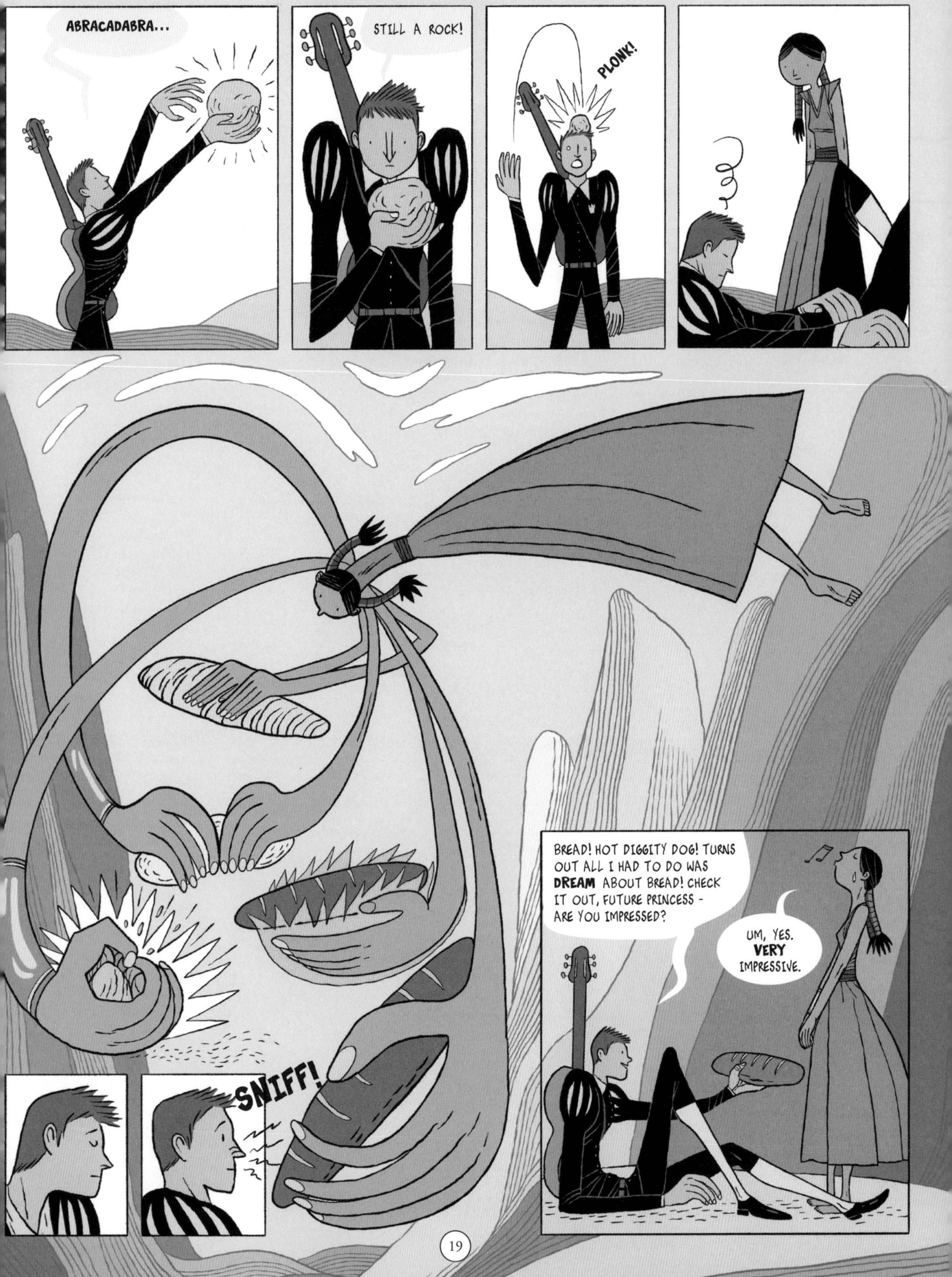
ABRACADABRA...
STILL A ROCK!
PLONK!
SNIFF!
BREAD! HOT DIGGITY DOG! TURNS OUT ALL I HAD TO DO WAS **DREAM** ABOUT BREAD! CHECK IT OUT, FUTURE PRINCESS - ARE YOU IMPRESSED?
UM, YES. **VERY** IMPRESSIVE.

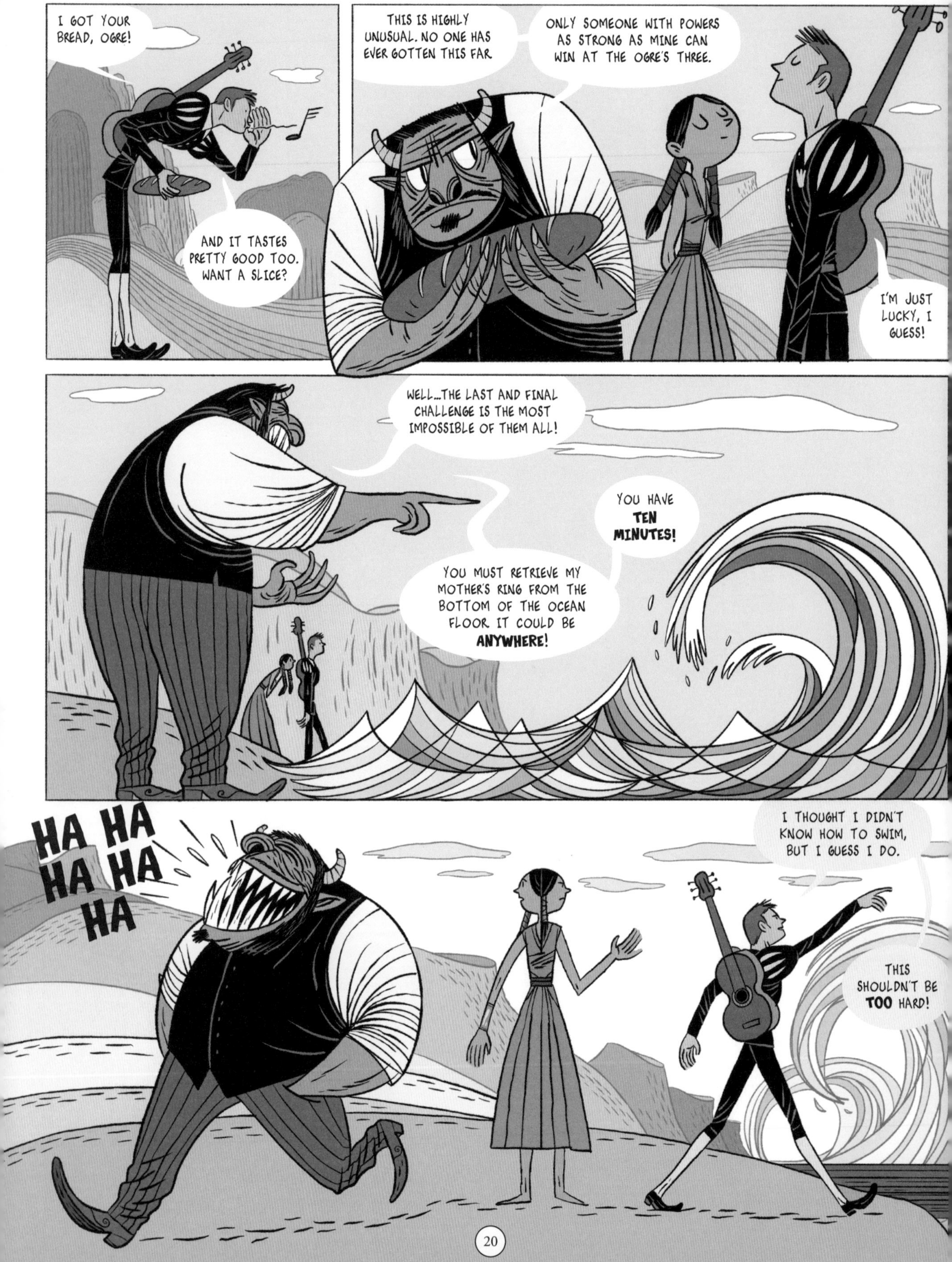

I GOT YOUR BREAD, OGRE!
AND IT TASTES PRETTY GOOD TOO. WANT A SLICE?
THIS IS HIGHLY UNUSUAL. NO ONE HAS EVER GOTTEN THIS FAR
ONLY SOMEONE WITH POWERS AS STRONG AS MINE CAN WIN AT THE OGRE'S THREE.
I'M JUST LUCKY, I GUESS!
WELL...THE LAST AND FINAL CHALLENGE IS THE MOST IMPOSSIBLE OF THEM ALL!
YOU MUST RETRIEVE MY MOTHER'S RING FROM THE BOTTOM OF THE OCEAN FLOOR IT COULD BE **ANYWHERE!**
YOU HAVE **TEN MINUTES!**
HA HA HA HA HA
I THOUGHT I DIDN'T KNOW HOW TO SWIM, BUT I GUESS I DO.
THIS SHOULDN'T BE **TOO** HARD!

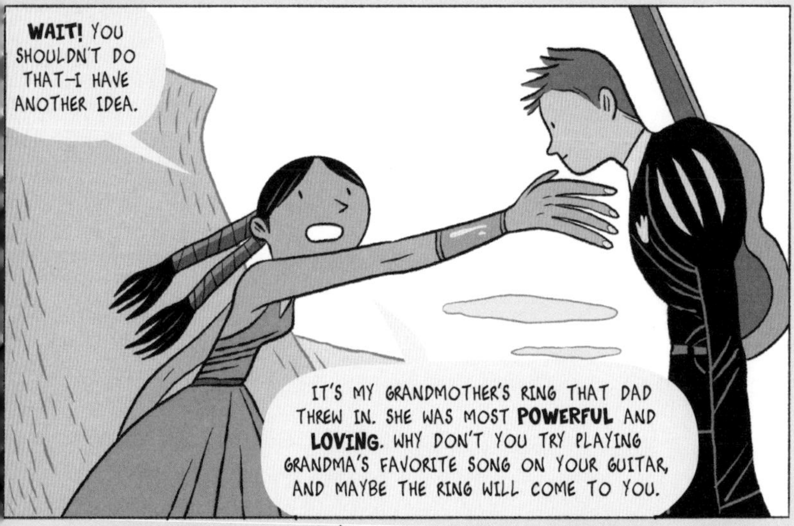
WAIT! YOU SHOULDN'T DO THAT—I HAVE ANOTHER IDEA.
IT'S MY GRANDMOTHER'S RING THAT DAD THREW IN. SHE WAS MOST POWERFUL AND LOVING. WHY DON'T YOU TRY PLAYING GRANDMA'S FAVORITE SONG ON YOUR GUITAR, AND MAYBE THE RING WILL COME TO YOU.

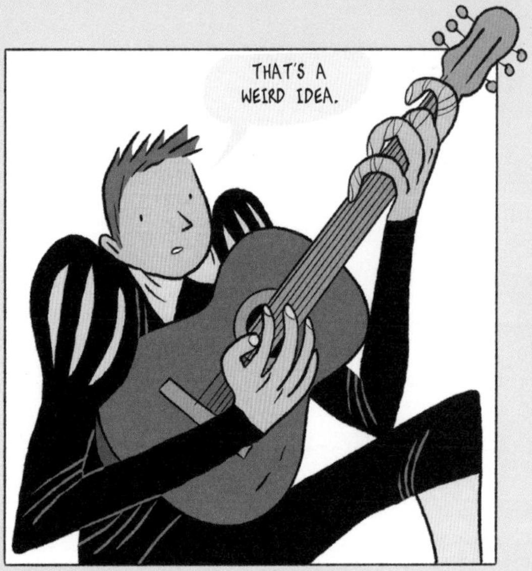
THAT'S A WEIRD IDEA.

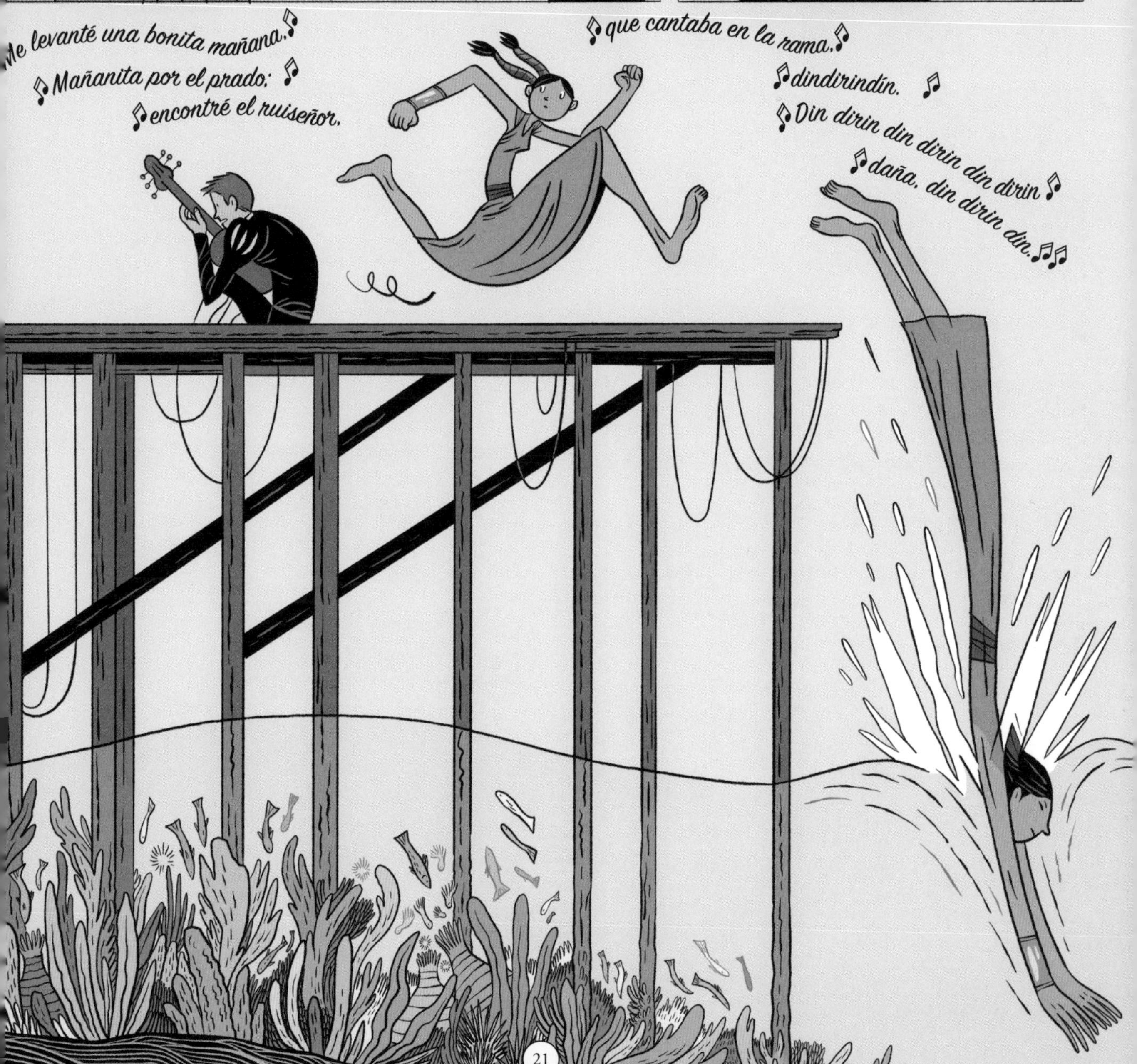
Me levanté una bonita mañana,
Mañanita por el prado;
encontré el ruiseñor,
que cantaba en la rama.
dindirindín.
Din dirin din dirin din dirin
daña, din dirin din.

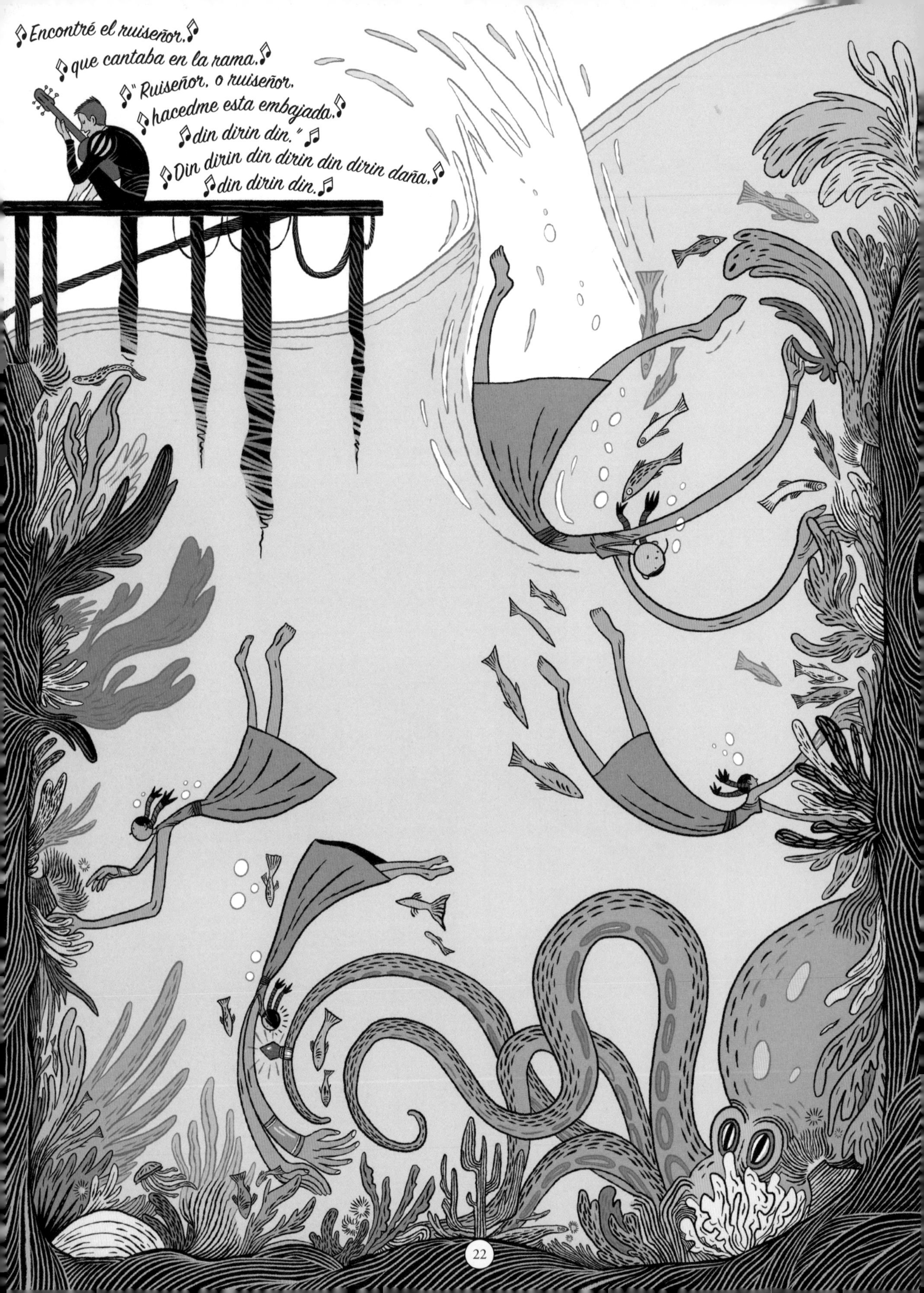
♪Encontré el ruiseñor,♪
♪que cantaba en la rama,♪
♪"Ruiseñor, o ruiseñor,
♪hacedme esta embajada,♪
♪din dirin din."♫
♪Din dirin din dirin din dirin daña,♪
♪din dirin din.♫

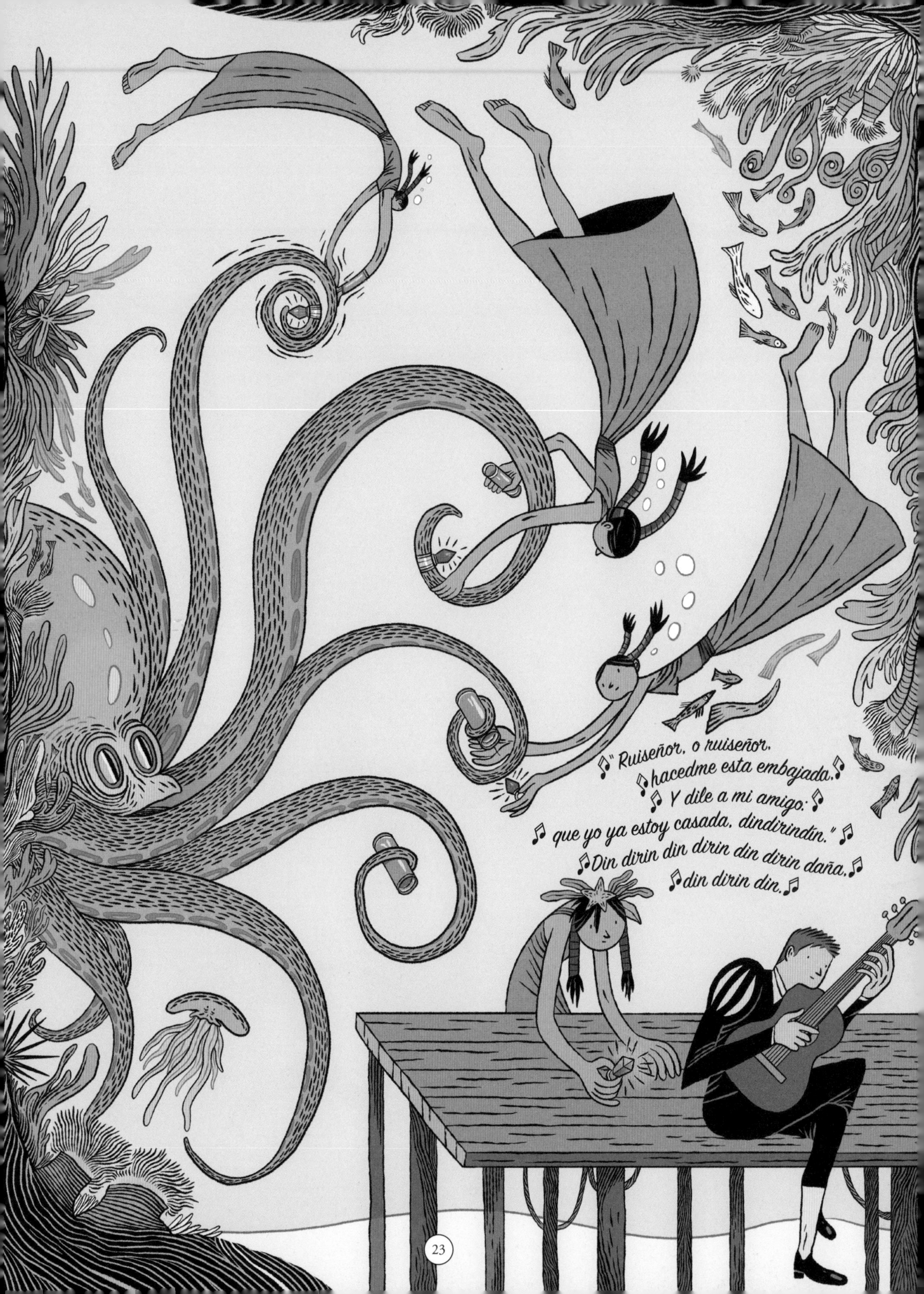
♫" Ruiseñor, o ruiseñor,
♫hacedme esta embajada.♫
♫ Y dile a mi amigo:♫
♫ que yo ya estoy casada, dindirindín."♫
♫Din dirin din dirin din dirin daña.♫
♫din dirin din.♫

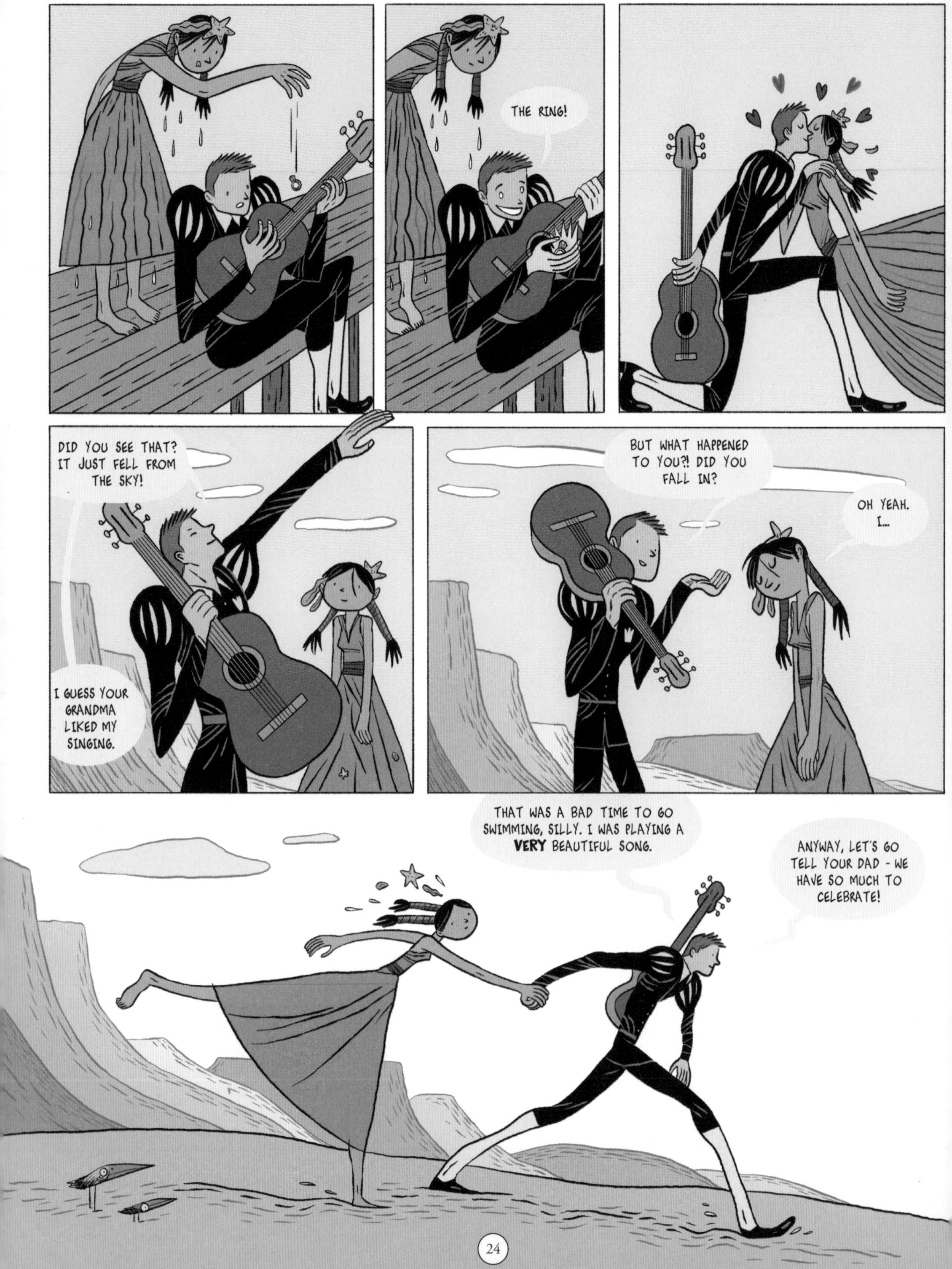

THE RING!
DID YOU SEE THAT? IT JUST FELL FROM THE SKY!
I GUESS YOUR GRANDMA LIKED MY SINGING.
BUT WHAT HAPPENED TO YOU?! DID YOU FALL IN?
OH YEAH. I...
THAT WAS A BAD TIME TO GO SWIMMING, SILLY. I WAS PLAYING A **VERY** BEAUTIFUL SONG.
ANYWAY, LET'S GO TELL YOUR DAD - WE HAVE SO MUCH TO CELEBRATE!

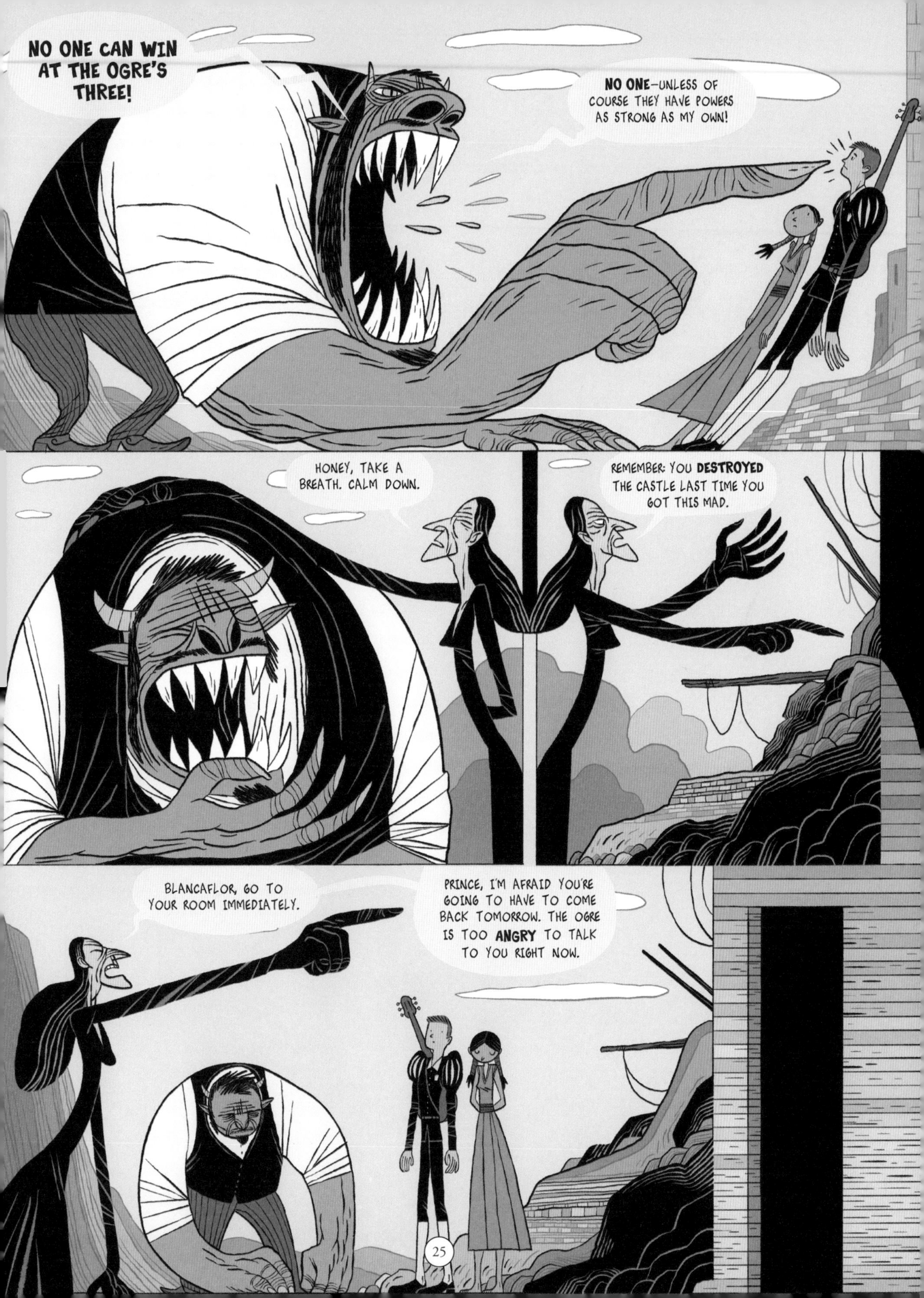
NO ONE CAN WIN AT THE OGRE'S THREE!
NO ONE—UNLESS OF COURSE THEY HAVE POWERS AS STRONG AS MY OWN!
HONEY, TAKE A BREATH. CALM DOWN.
REMEMBER: YOU DESTROYED THE CASTLE LAST TIME YOU GOT THIS MAD.
BLANCAFLOR, GO TO YOUR ROOM IMMEDIATELY.
PRINCE, I'M AFRAID YOU'RE GOING TO HAVE TO COME BACK TOMORROW. THE OGRE IS TOO ANGRY TO TALK TO YOU RIGHT NOW.

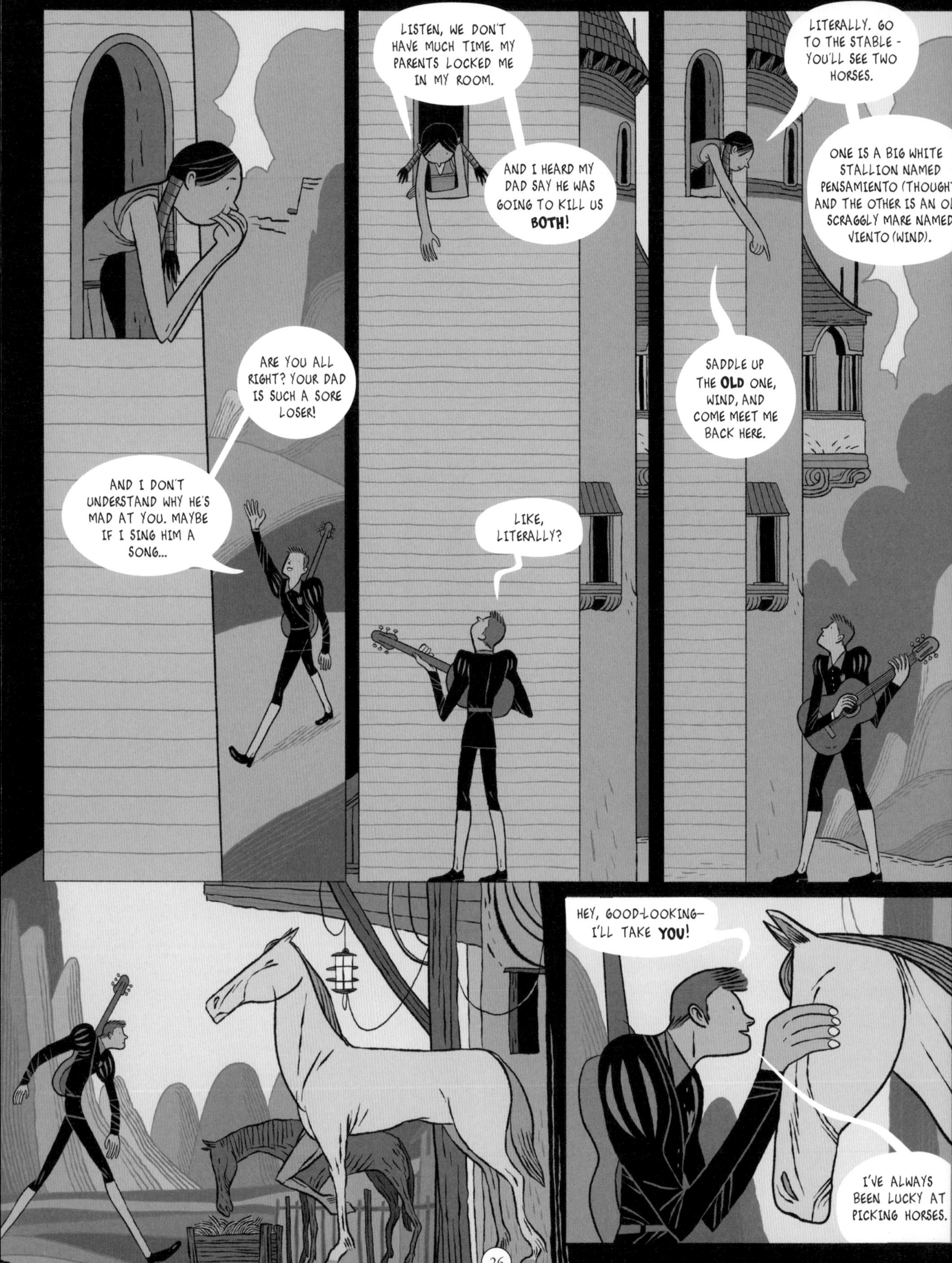

ARE YOU ALL RIGHT? YOUR DAD IS SUCH A SORE LOSER!
AND I DON'T UNDERSTAND WHY HE'S MAD AT YOU. MAYBE IF I SING HIM A SONG...
LISTEN, WE DON'T HAVE MUCH TIME. MY PARENTS LOCKED ME IN MY ROOM.
AND I HEARD MY DAD SAY HE WAS GOING TO KILL US **BOTH**!
LIKE, LITERALLY?
LITERALLY. GO TO THE STABLE - YOU'LL SEE TWO HORSES.
ONE IS A BIG WHITE STALLION NAMED PENSAMIENTO (THOUGHT) AND THE OTHER IS AN OLD SCRAGGLY MARE NAMED VIENTO (WIND).
SADDLE UP THE **OLD** ONE, WIND, AND COME MEET ME BACK HERE.
HEY, GOOD-LOOKING— I'LL TAKE **YOU**!
I'VE ALWAYS BEEN LUCKY AT PICKING HORSES.

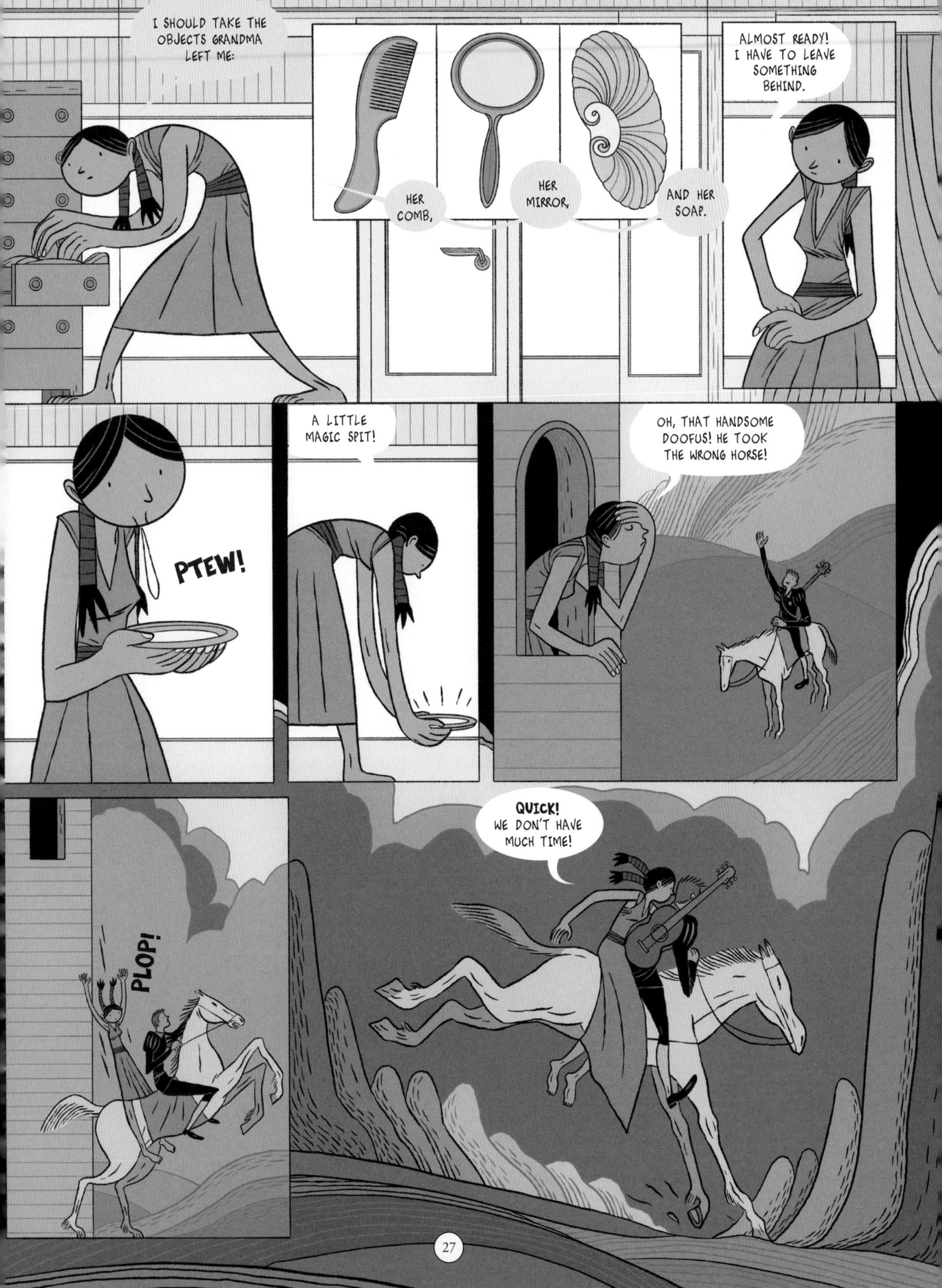
I SHOULD TAKE THE OBJECTS GRANDMA LEFT ME:
HER COMB,
HER MIRROR,
AND HER SOAP.
ALMOST READY! I HAVE TO LEAVE SOMETHING BEHIND.
PTEW!
A LITTLE MAGIC SPIT!
OH, THAT HANDSOME DOOFUS! HE TOOK THE WRONG HORSE!
PLOP!
QUICK! WE DON'T HAVE MUCH TIME!

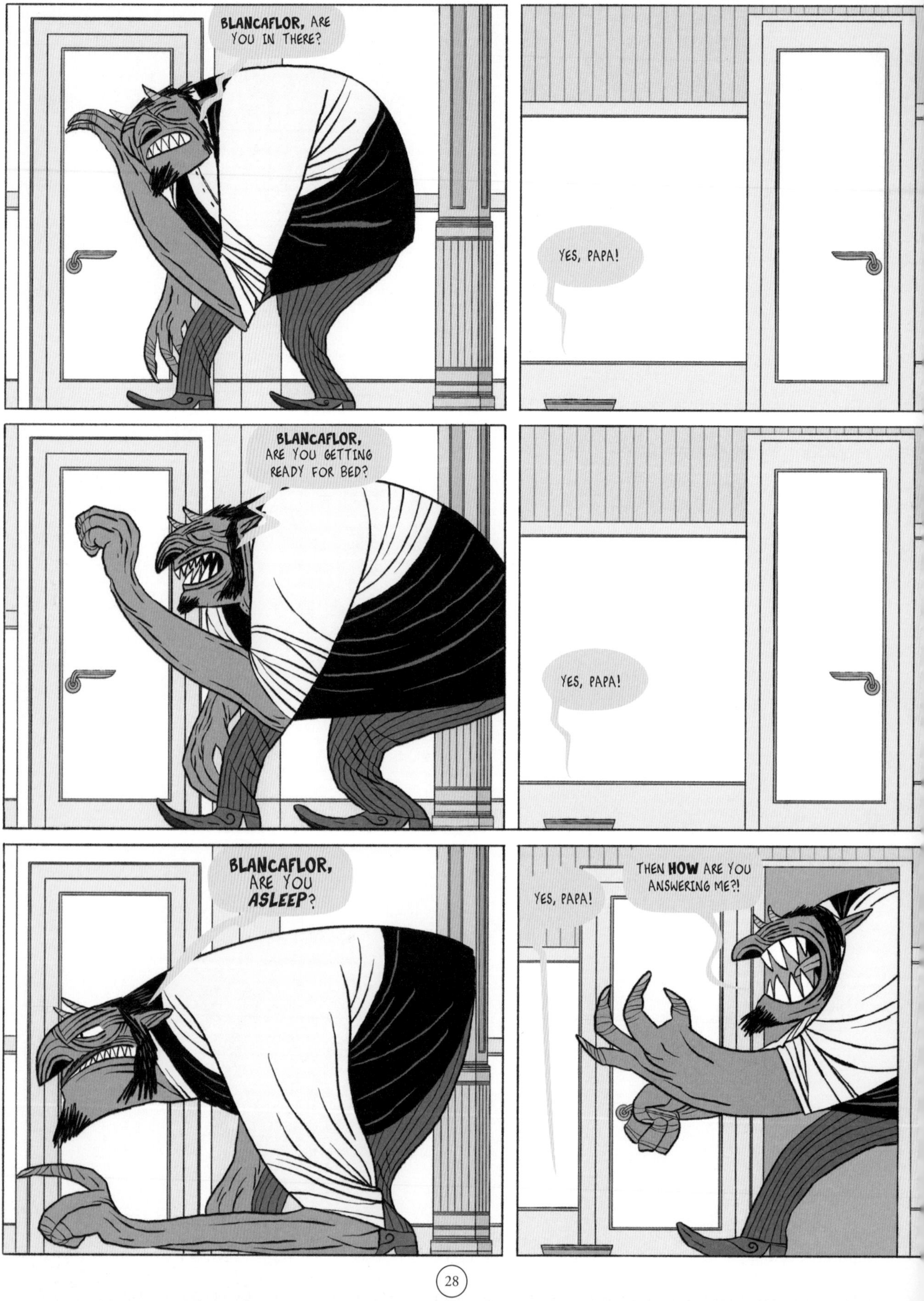
BLANCAFLOR, ARE YOU IN THERE?
YES, PAPA!
BLANCAFLOR, ARE YOU GETTING READY FOR BED?
YES, PAPA!
BLANCAFLOR, ARE YOU ASLEEP?
YES, PAPA!
THEN HOW ARE YOU ANSWERING ME?!

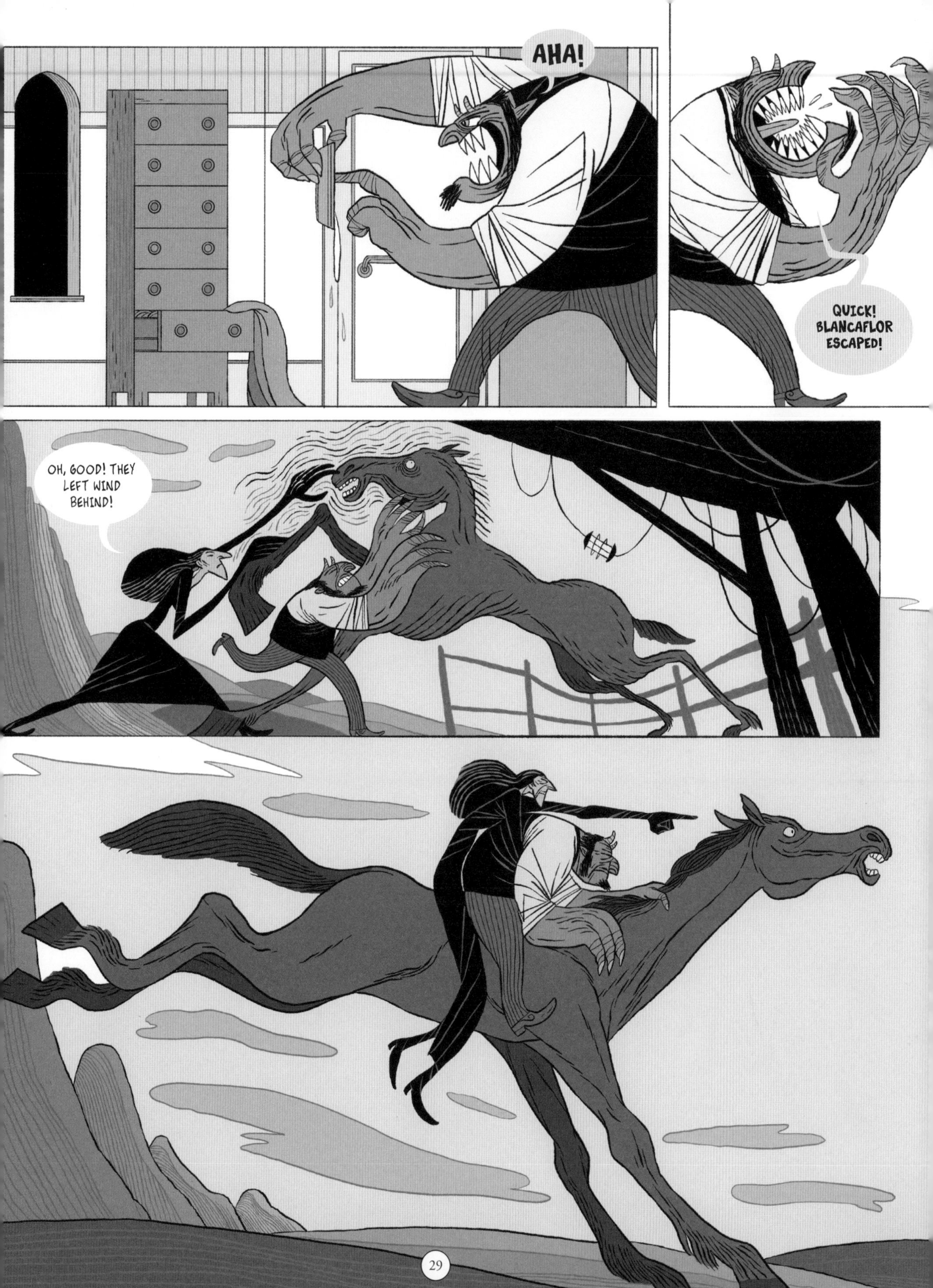
AHA!
QUICK! BLANCAFLOR ESCAPED!
OH, GOOD! THEY LEFT WIND BEHIND!

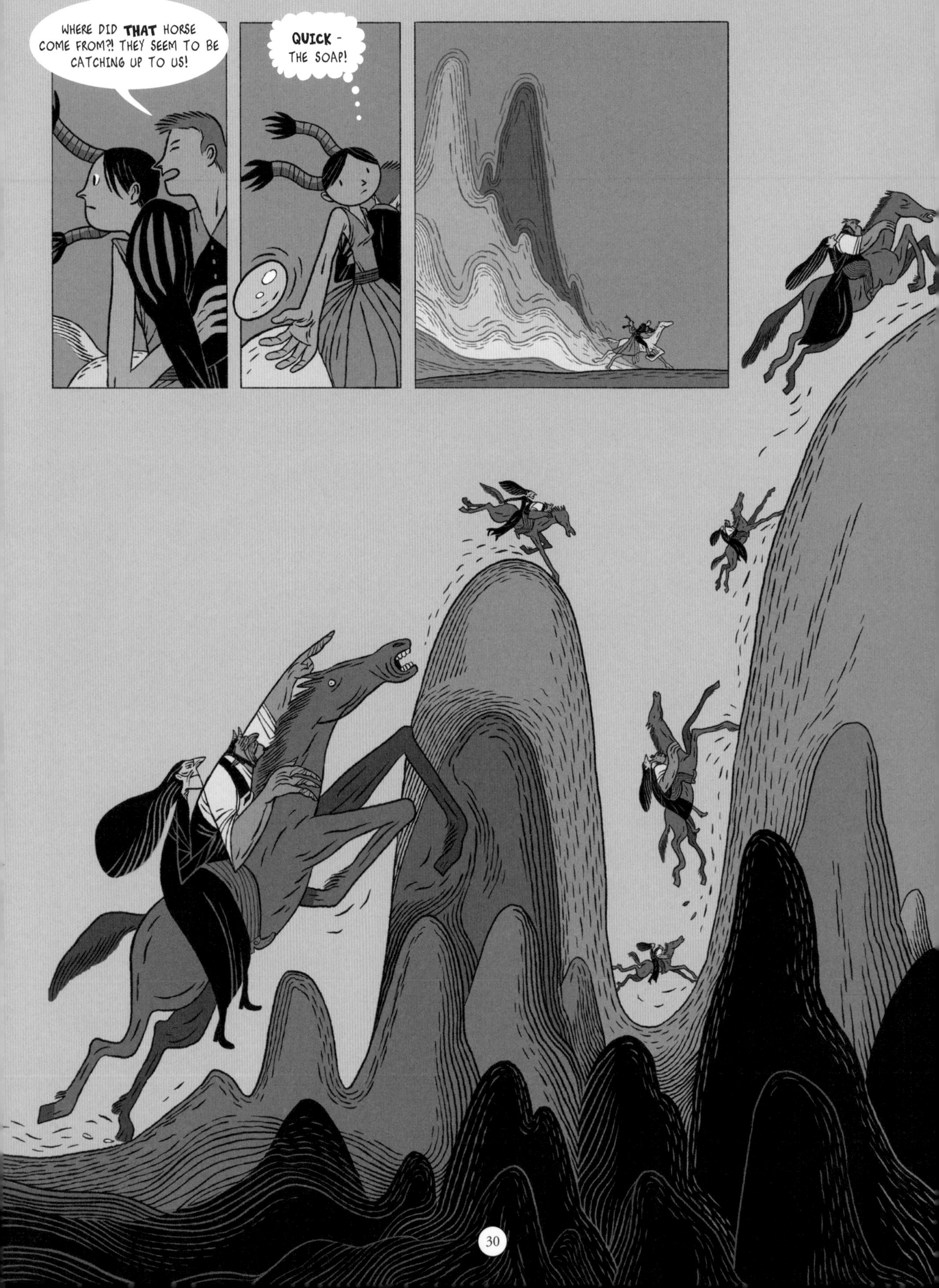
WHERE DID THAT HORSE COME FROM?! THEY SEEM TO BE CATCHING UP TO US!
QUICK - THE SOAP!

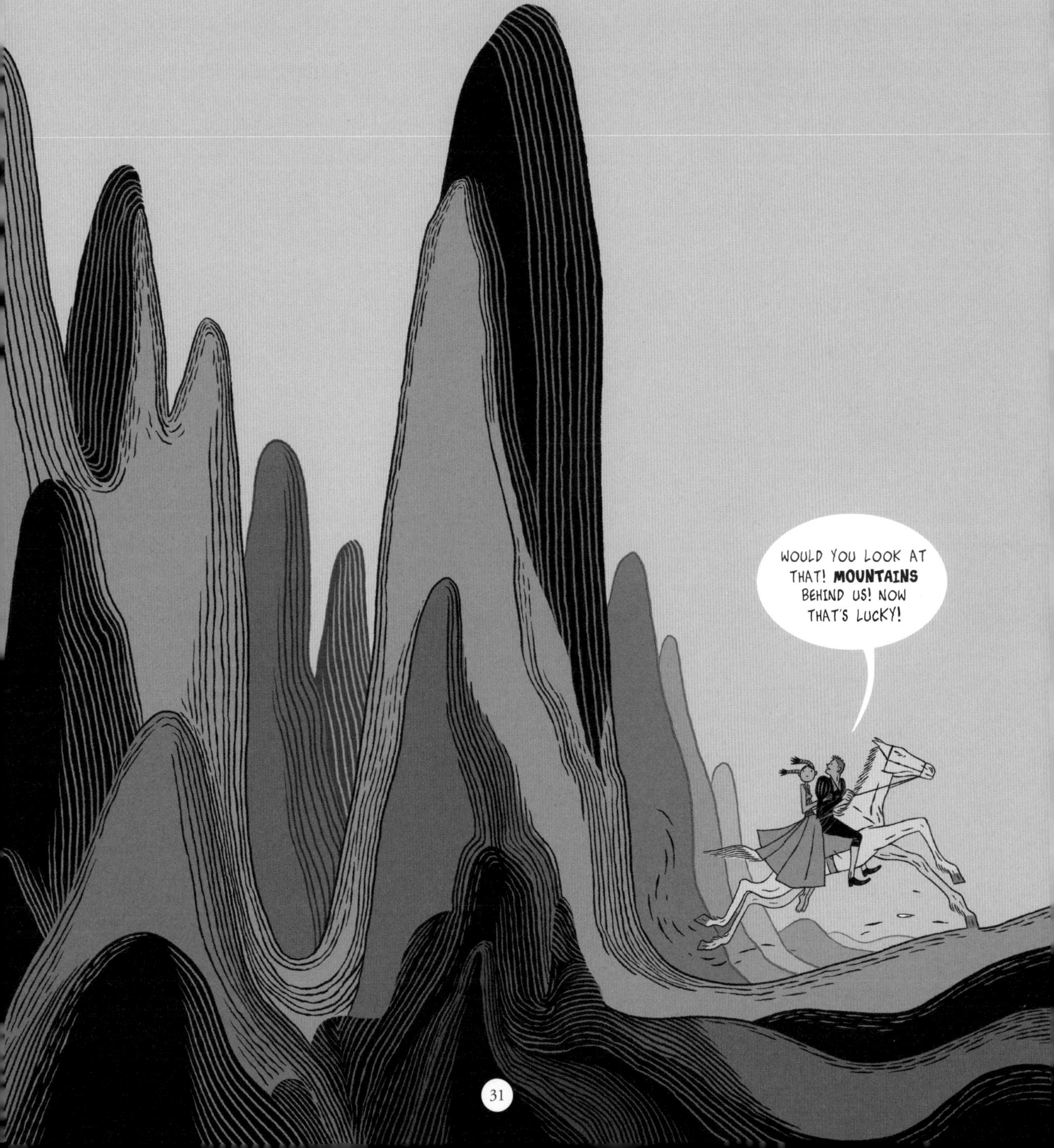
WOULD YOU LOOK AT THAT! **MOUNTAINS** BEHIND US! NOW THAT'S LUCKY!

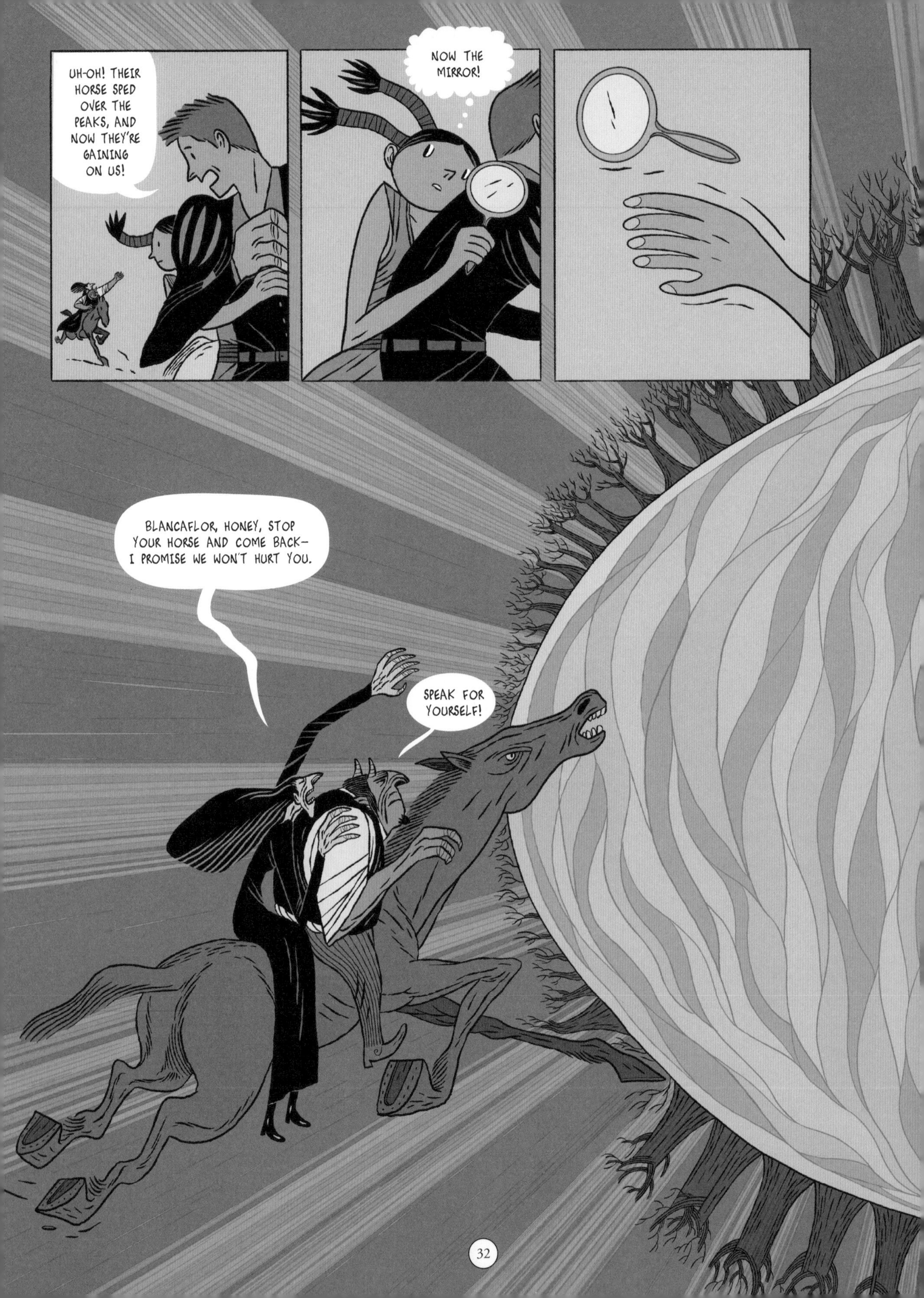
UH-OH! THEIR HORSE SPED OVER THE PEAKS, AND NOW THEY'RE GAINING ON US!
NOW THE MIRROR!
BLANCAFLOR, HONEY, STOP YOUR HORSE AND COME BACK— I PROMISE WE WON'T HURT YOU.
SPEAK FOR YOURSELF!

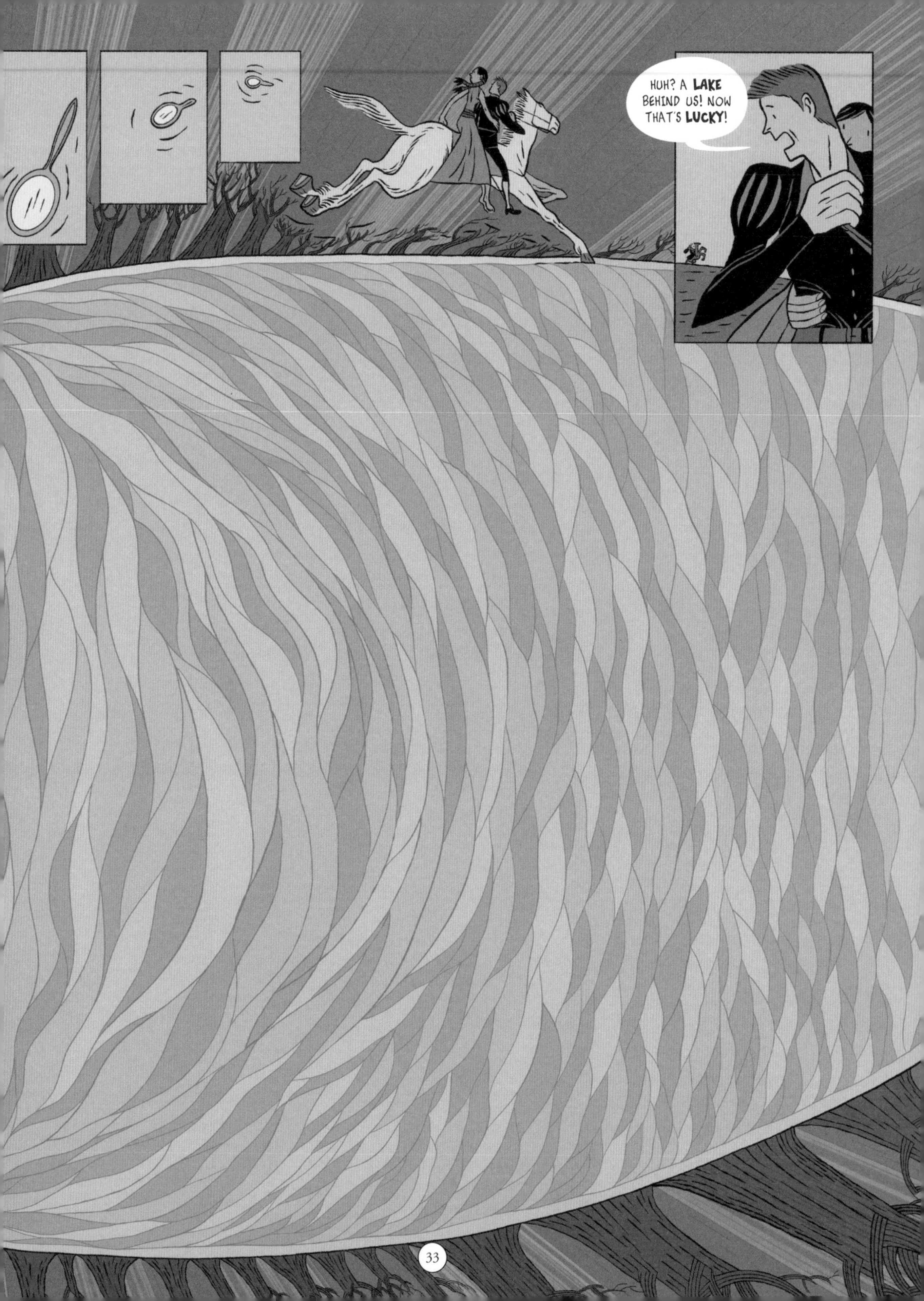
HUH? A LAKE BEHIND US! NOW THAT'S LUCKY!

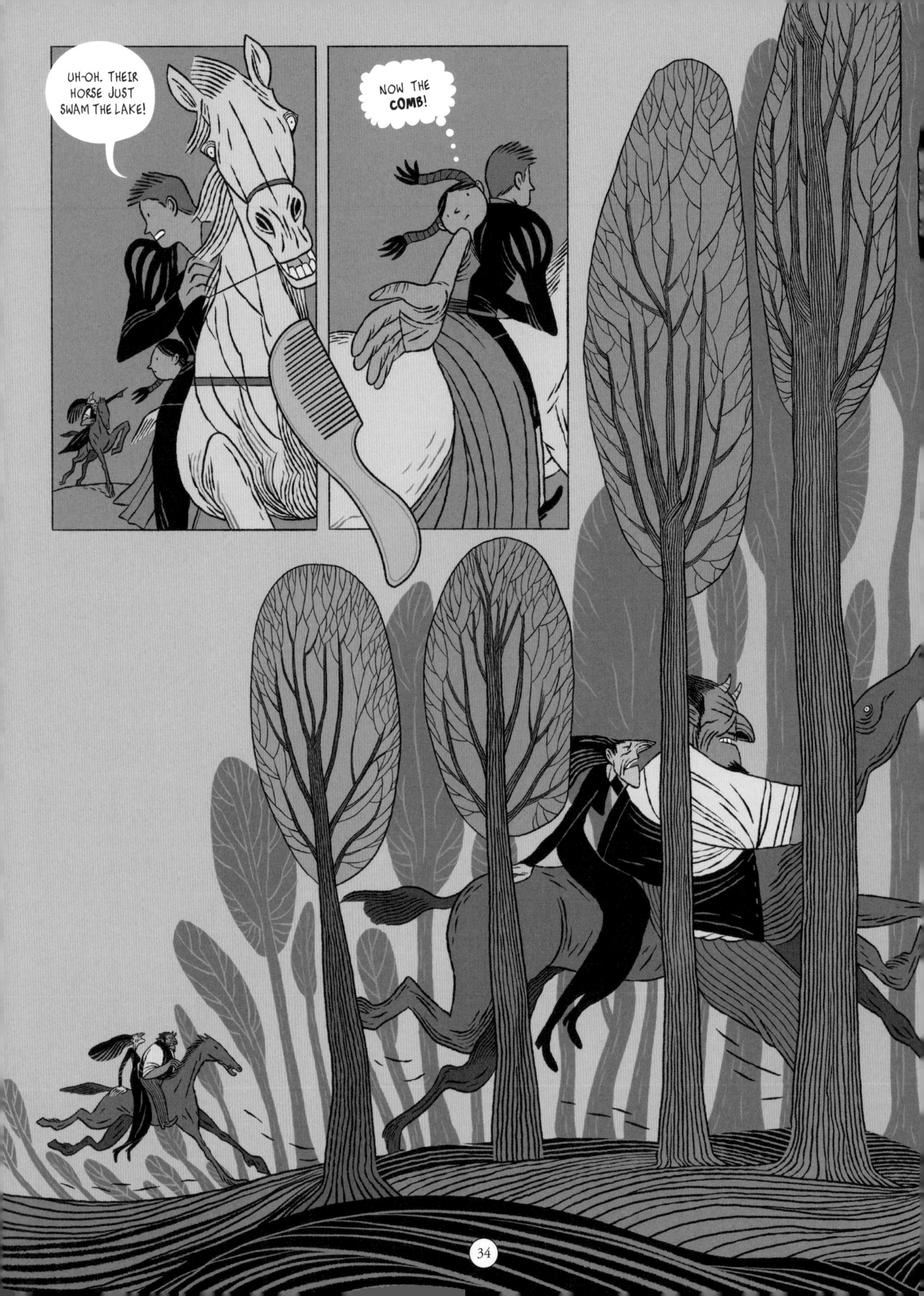
UH-OH. THEIR HORSE JUST SWAM THE LAKE!
NOW THE COMB!

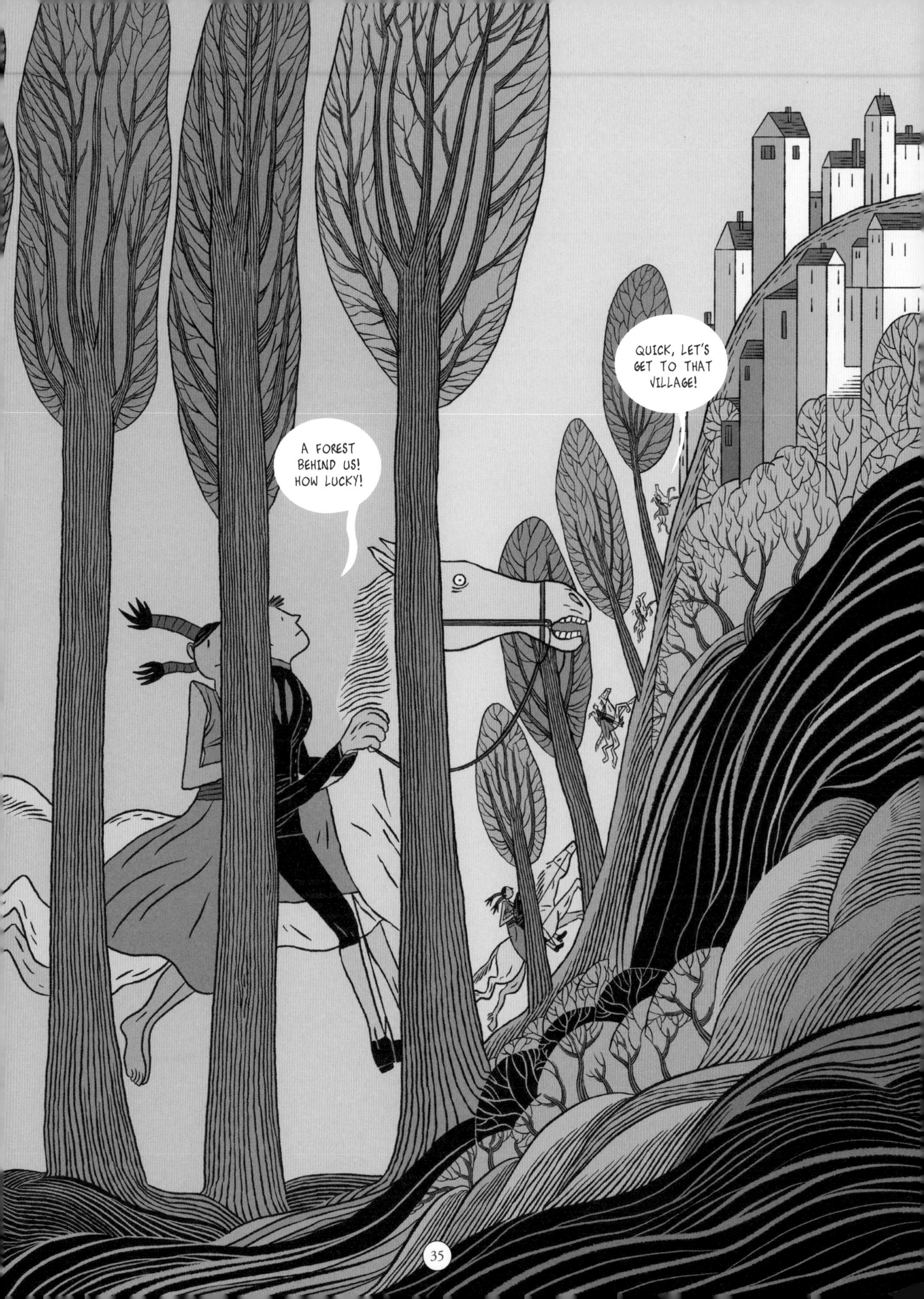
A FOREST BEHIND US! HOW LUCKY!
QUICK, LET'S GET TO THAT VILLAGE!

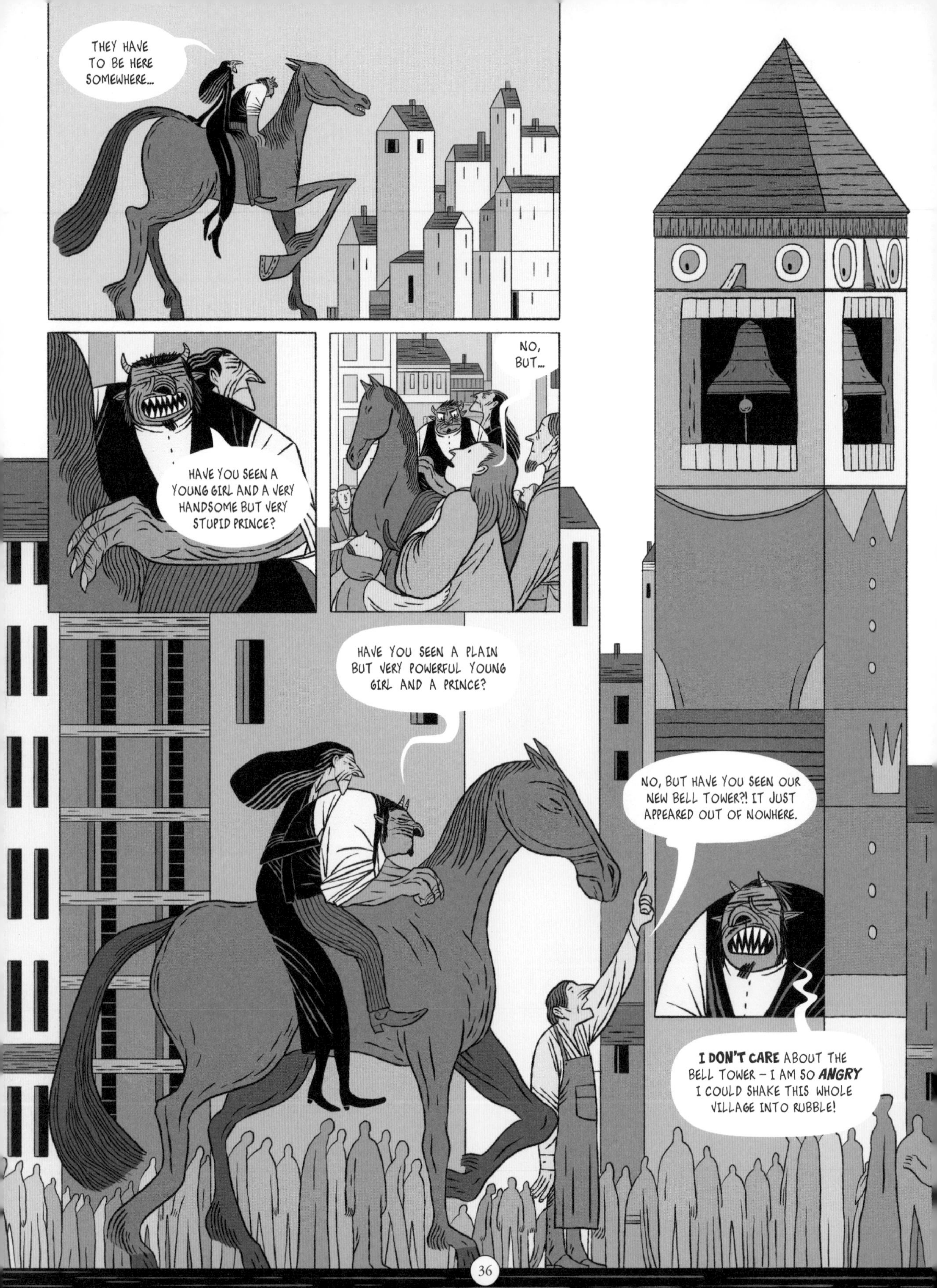

THEY HAVE TO BE HERE SOMEWHERE...
HAVE YOU SEEN A YOUNG GIRL AND A VERY HANDSOME BUT VERY STUPID PRINCE?
NO, BUT...
HAVE YOU SEEN A PLAIN BUT VERY POWERFUL YOUNG GIRL AND A PRINCE?
NO, BUT HAVE YOU SEEN OUR NEW BELL TOWER?! IT JUST APPEARED OUT OF NOWHERE.
I DON'T CARE ABOUT THE BELL TOWER – I AM SO ANGRY I COULD SHAKE THIS WHOLE VILLAGE INTO RUBBLE!

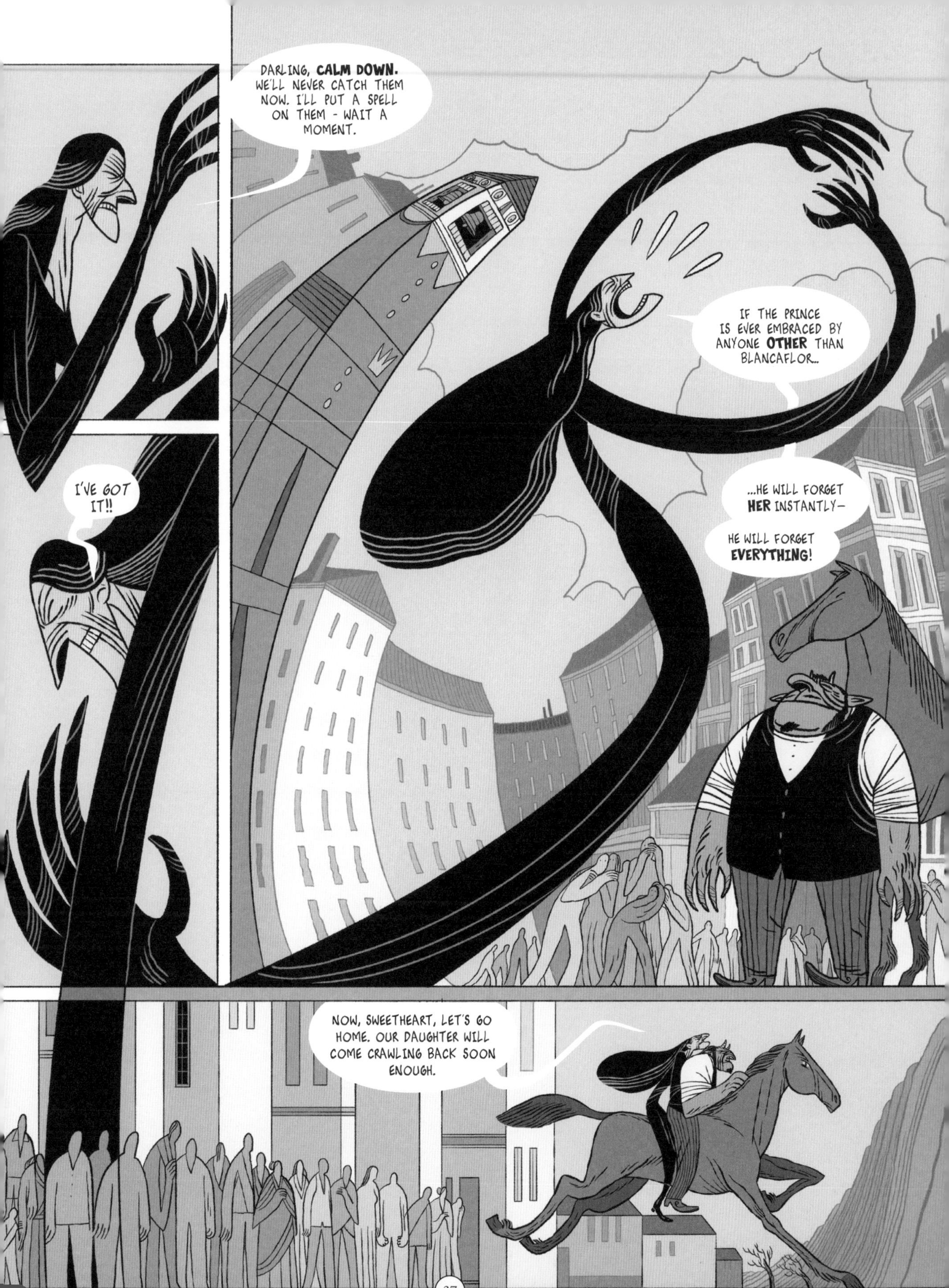

DARLING, CALM DOWN. WE'LL NEVER CATCH THEM NOW. I'LL PUT A SPELL ON THEM - WAIT A MOMENT.
I'VE GOT IT!!
IF THE PRINCE IS EVER EMBRACED BY ANYONE OTHER THAN BLANCAFLOR...
...HE WILL FORGET HER INSTANTLY—
HE WILL FORGET EVERYTHING!
NOW, SWEETHEART, LET'S GO HOME. OUR DAUGHTER WILL COME CRAWLING BACK SOON ENOUGH.

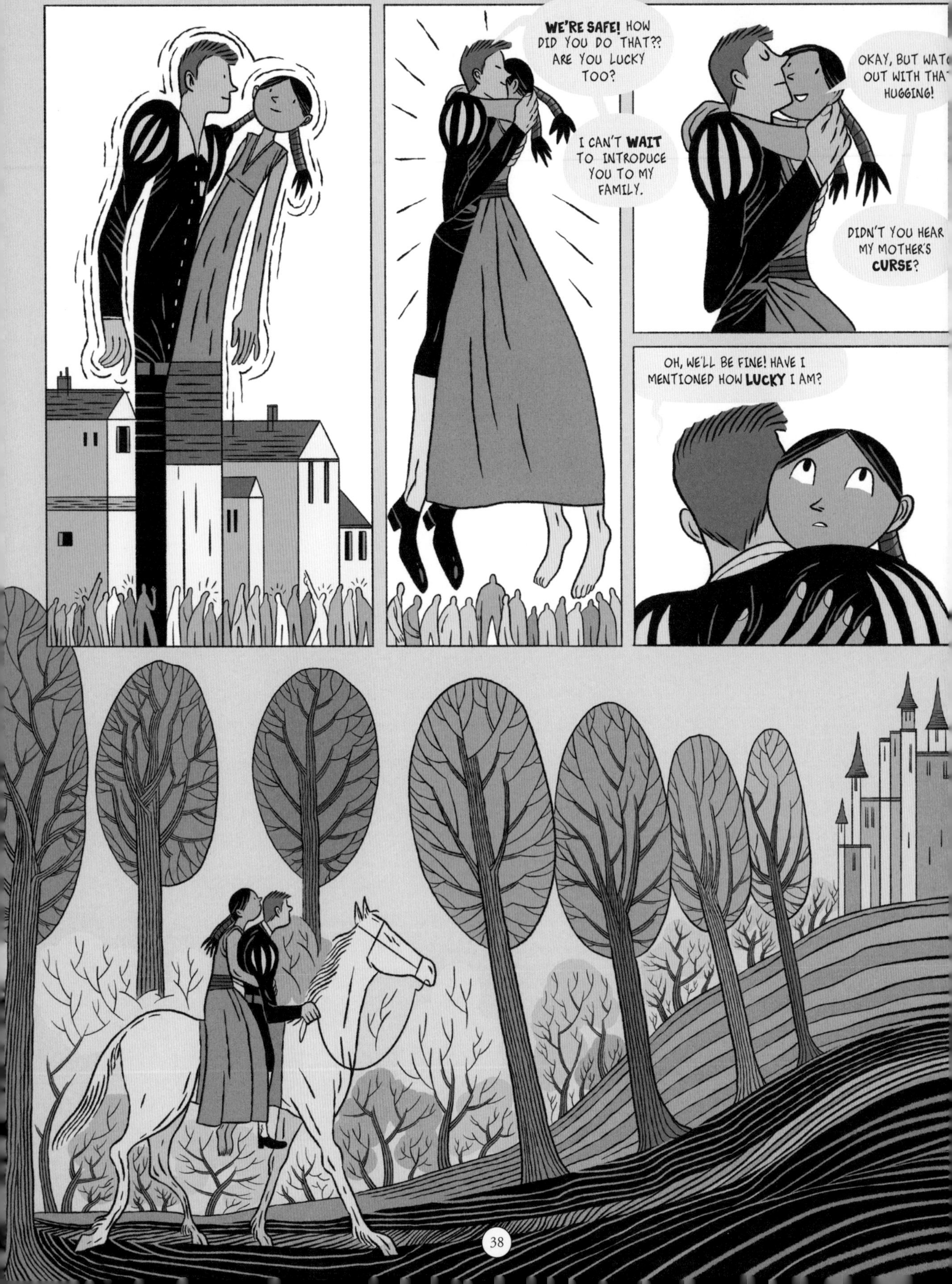

WE'RE SAFE! HOW DID YOU DO THAT?? ARE YOU LUCKY TOO?
I CAN'T WAIT TO INTRODUCE YOU TO MY FAMILY.
OKAY, BUT WATC OUT WITH THAT HUGGING!
DIDN'T YOU HEAR MY MOTHER'S CURSE?
OH, WE'LL BE FINE! HAVE I MENTIONED HOW LUCKY I AM?

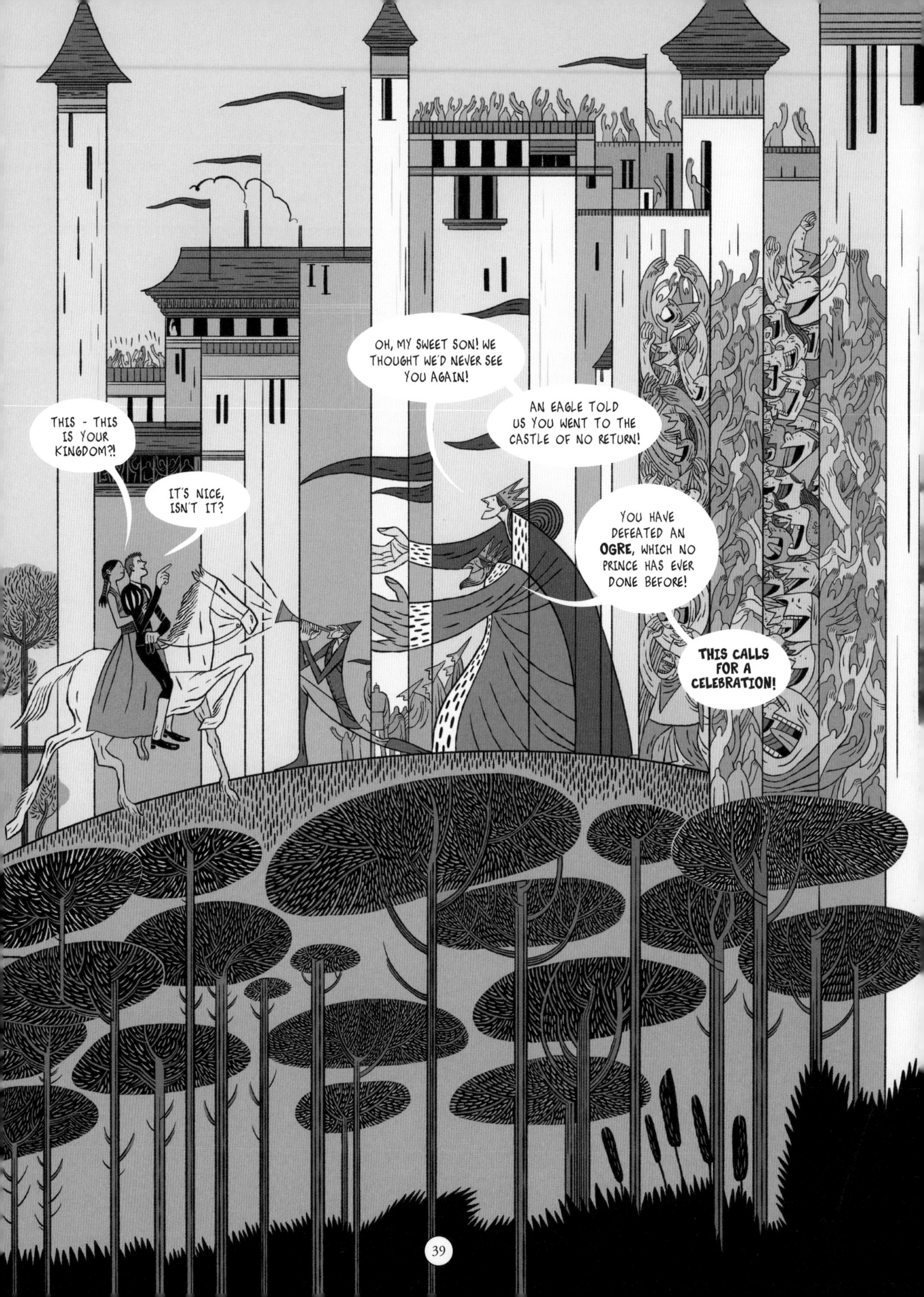
THIS - THIS IS YOUR KINGDOM?!
IT'S NICE, ISN'T IT?
OH, MY SWEET SON! WE THOUGHT WE'D NEVER SEE YOU AGAIN!
AN EAGLE TOLD US YOU WENT TO THE CASTLE OF NO RETURN!
YOU HAVE DEFEATED AN **OGRE**, WHICH NO PRINCE HAS EVER DONE BEFORE!
THIS CALLS FOR A CELEBRATION!

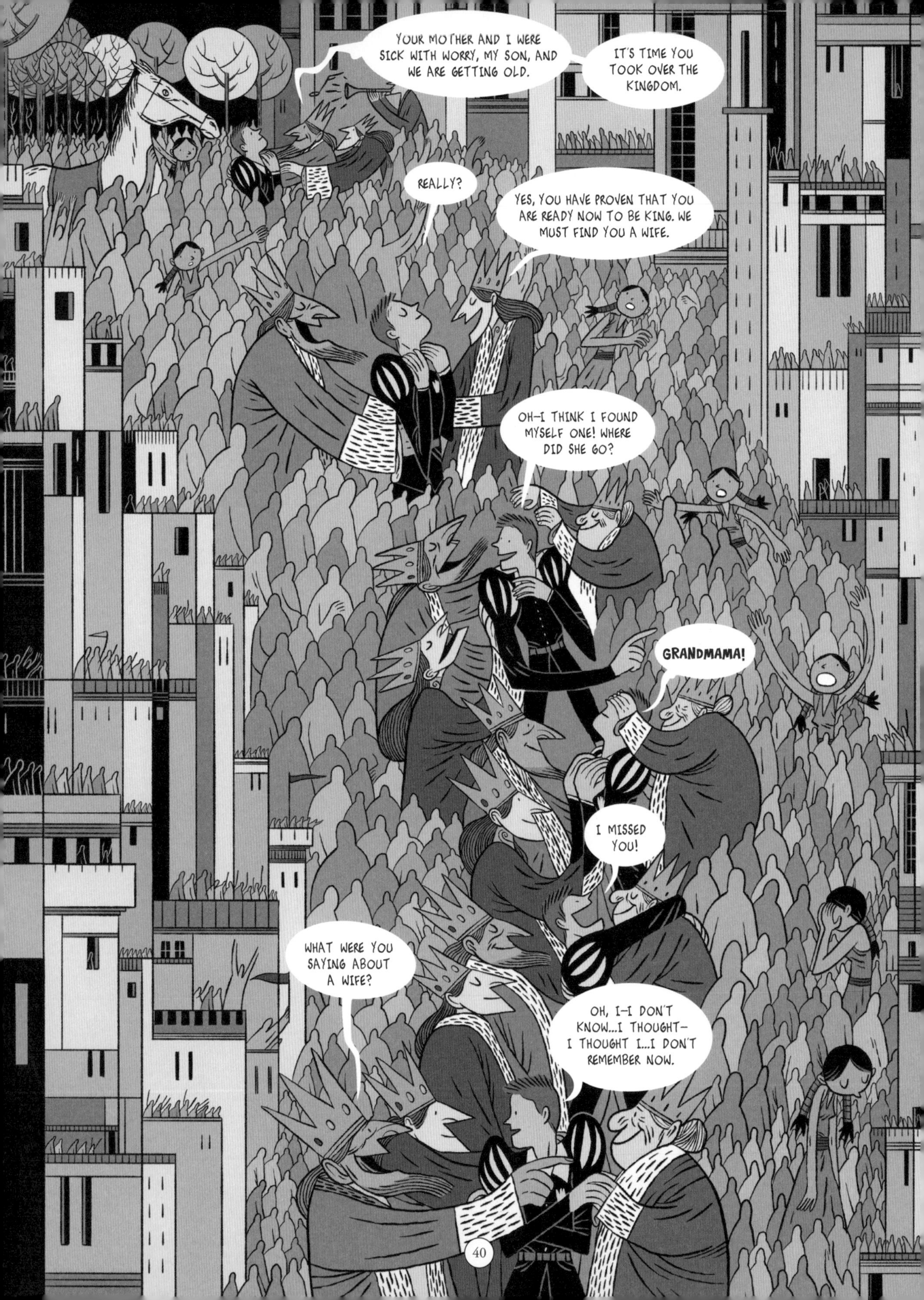
YOUR MOTHER AND I WERE SICK WITH WORRY, MY SON, AND WE ARE GETTING OLD.
IT'S TIME YOU TOOK OVER THE KINGDOM.
REALLY?
YES, YOU HAVE PROVEN THAT YOU ARE READY NOW TO BE KING. WE MUST FIND YOU A WIFE.
OH—I THINK I FOUND MYSELF ONE! WHERE DID SHE GO?
GRANDMAMA!
I MISSED YOU!
WHAT WERE YOU SAYING ABOUT A WIFE?
OH, I—I DON'T KNOW...I THOUGHT— I THOUGHT I...I DON'T REMEMBER NOW.

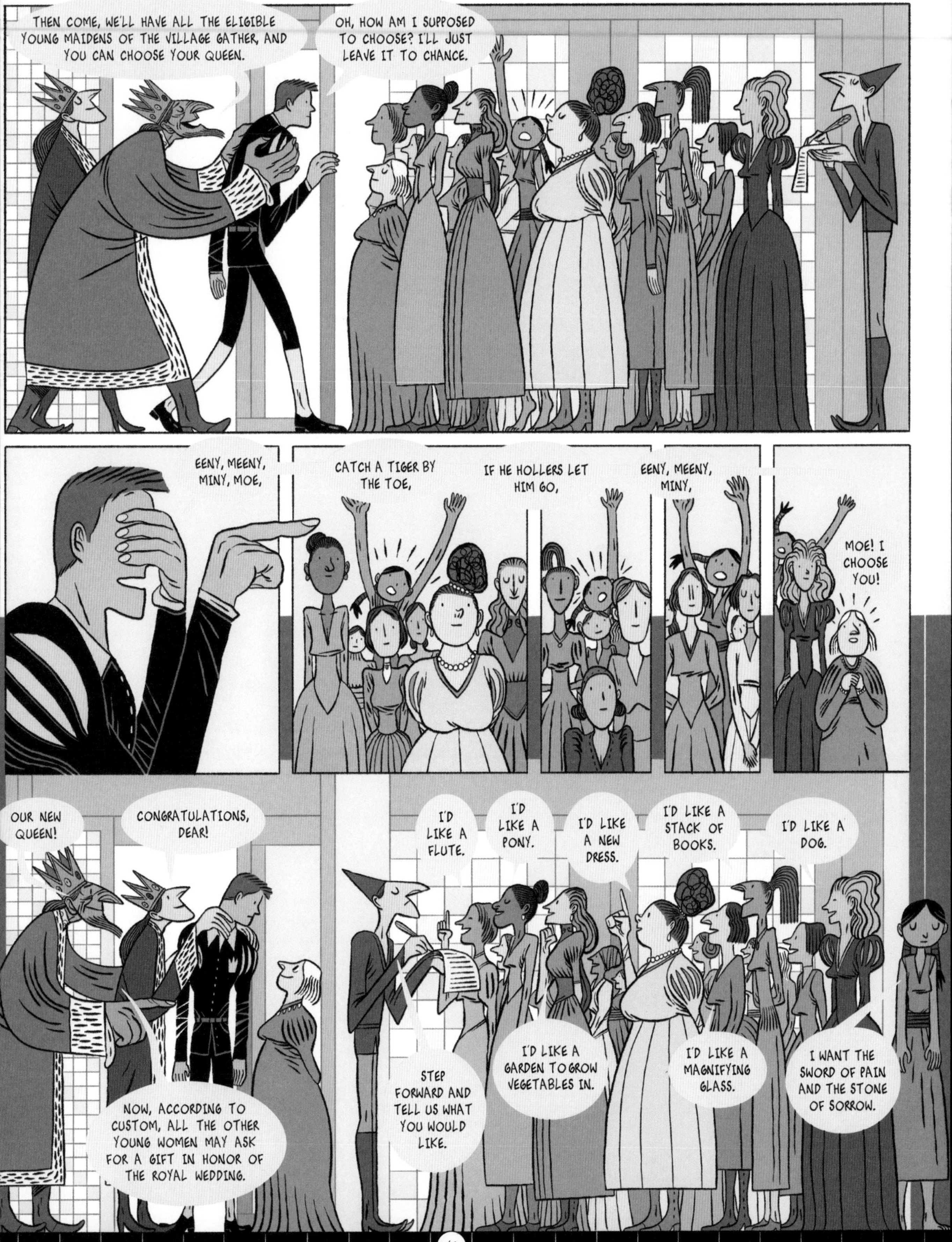

THEN COME, WE'LL HAVE ALL THE ELIGIBLE YOUNG MAIDENS OF THE VILLAGE GATHER, AND YOU CAN CHOOSE YOUR QUEEN.
OH, HOW AM I SUPPOSED TO CHOOSE? I'LL JUST LEAVE IT TO CHANCE.
EENY, MEENY, MINY, MOE,
CATCH A TIGER BY THE TOE,
IF HE HOLLERS LET HIM GO,
EENY, MEENY, MINY,
MOE! I CHOOSE YOU!
OUR NEW QUEEN!
CONGRATULATIONS, DEAR!
NOW, ACCORDING TO CUSTOM, ALL THE OTHER YOUNG WOMEN MAY ASK FOR A GIFT IN HONOR OF THE ROYAL WEDDING.
STEP FORWARD AND TELL US WHAT YOU WOULD LIKE.
I'D LIKE A FLUTE.
I'D LIKE A PONY.
I'D LIKE A NEW DRESS.
I'D LIKE A GARDEN TO GROW VEGETABLES IN.
I'D LIKE A STACK OF BOOKS.
I'D LIKE A MAGNIFYING GLASS.
I'D LIKE A DOG.
I WANT THE SWORD OF PAIN AND THE STONE OF SORROW.

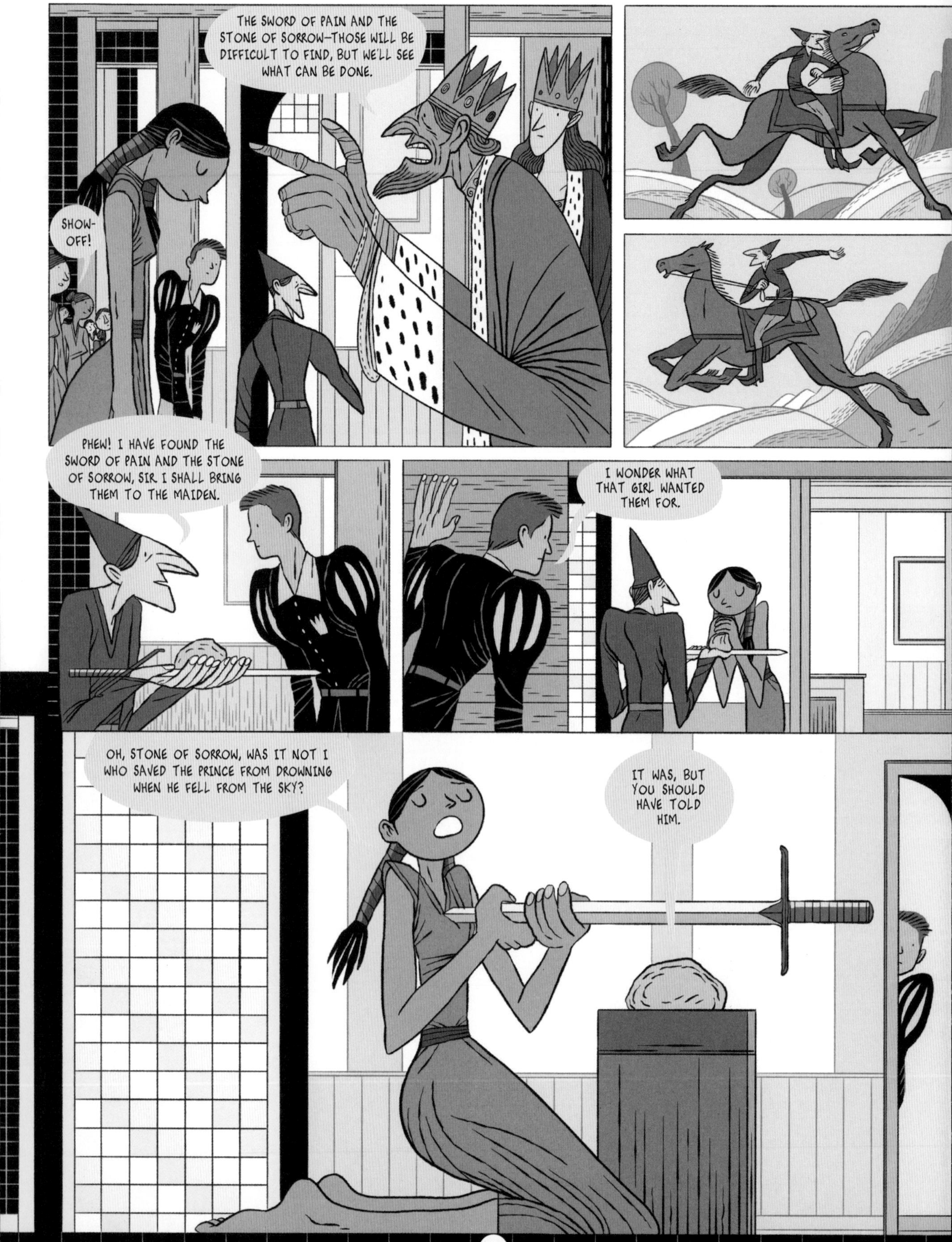
THE SWORD OF PAIN AND THE STONE OF SORROW—THOSE WILL BE DIFFICULT TO FIND, BUT WE'LL SEE WHAT CAN BE DONE.
SHOW-OFF!
PHEW! I HAVE FOUND THE SWORD OF PAIN AND THE STONE OF SORROW, SIR. I SHALL BRING THEM TO THE MAIDEN.
I WONDER WHAT THAT GIRL WANTED THEM FOR.
OH, STONE OF SORROW, WAS IT NOT I WHO SAVED THE PRINCE FROM DROWNING WHEN HE FELL FROM THE SKY?
IT WAS, BUT YOU SHOULD HAVE TOLD HIM.

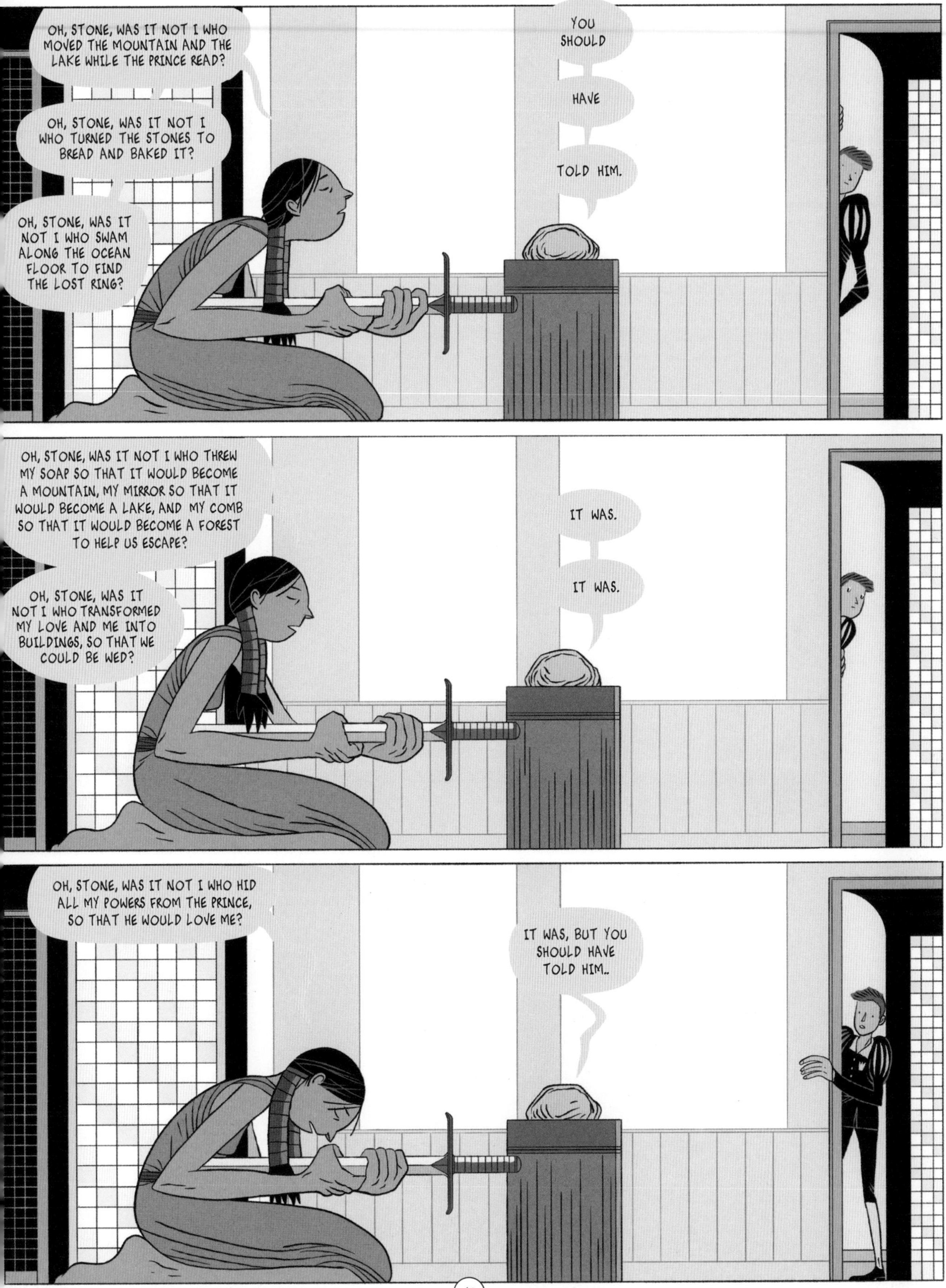
OH, STONE, WAS IT NOT I WHO MOVED THE MOUNTAIN AND THE LAKE WHILE THE PRINCE READ?
YOU SHOULD
OH, STONE, WAS IT NOT I WHO TURNED THE STONES TO BREAD AND BAKED IT?
HAVE
OH, STONE, WAS IT NOT I WHO SWAM ALONG THE OCEAN FLOOR TO FIND THE LOST RING?
TOLD HIM.
OH, STONE, WAS IT NOT I WHO THREW MY SOAP SO THAT IT WOULD BECOME A MOUNTAIN, MY MIRROR SO THAT IT WOULD BECOME A LAKE, AND MY COMB SO THAT IT WOULD BECOME A FOREST TO HELP US ESCAPE?
IT WAS.
OH, STONE, WAS IT NOT I WHO TRANSFORMED MY LOVE AND ME INTO BUILDINGS, SO THAT WE COULD BE WED?
IT WAS.
OH, STONE, WAS IT NOT I WHO HID ALL MY POWERS FROM THE PRINCE, SO THAT HE WOULD LOVE ME?
IT WAS, BUT YOU SHOULD HAVE TOLD HIM..

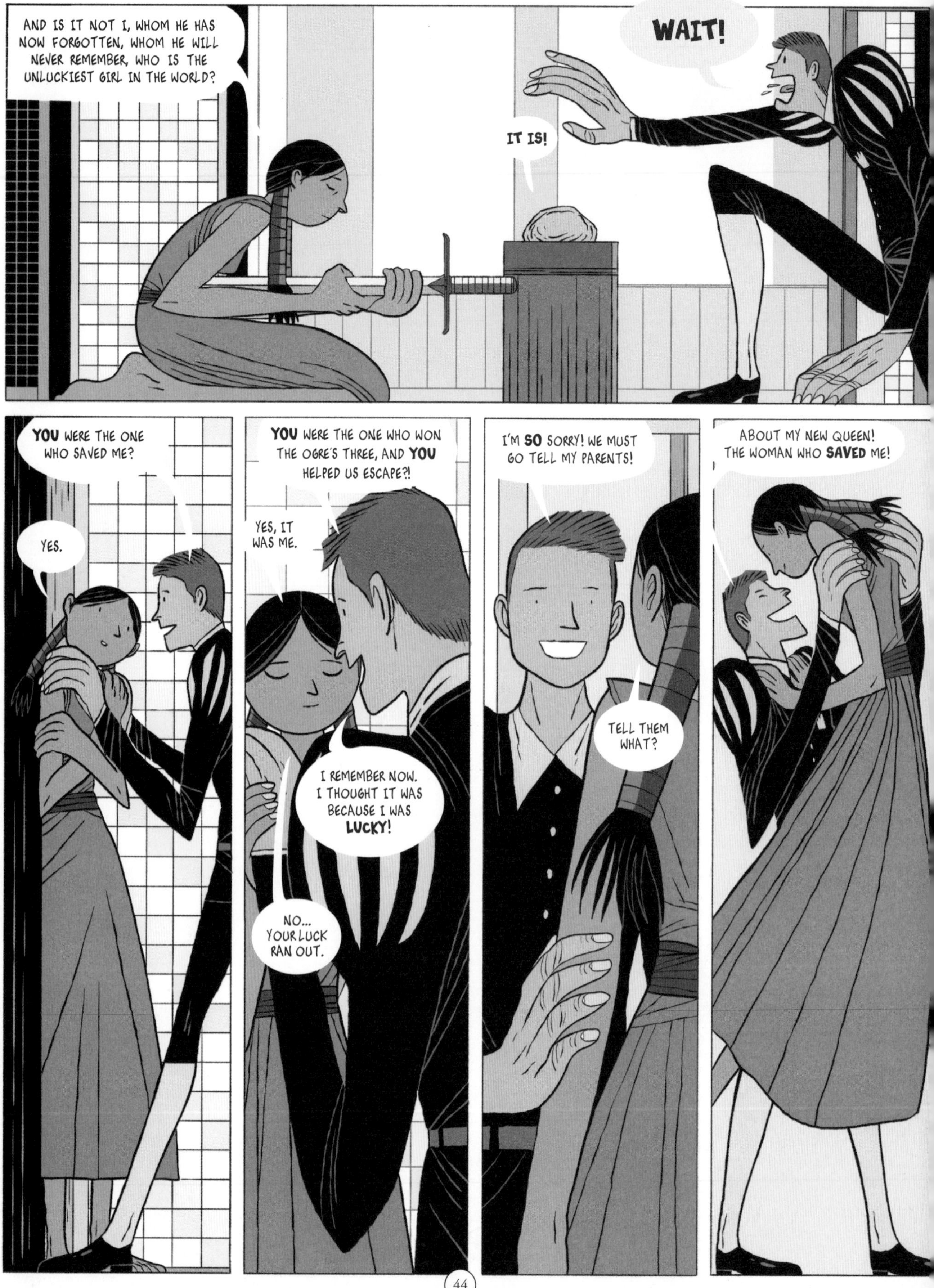
AND IS IT NOT I, WHOM HE HAS NOW FORGOTTEN, WHOM HE WILL NEVER REMEMBER, WHO IS THE UNLUCKIEST GIRL IN THE WORLD?
WAIT!
IT IS!
YOU WERE THE ONE WHO SAVED ME?
YES.
YOU WERE THE ONE WHO WON THE OGRE'S THREE, AND YOU HELPED US ESCAPE?!
YES, IT WAS ME.
I REMEMBER NOW. I THOUGHT IT WAS BECAUSE I WAS LUCKY!
NO... YOUR LUCK RAN OUT.
I'M SO SORRY! WE MUST GO TELL MY PARENTS!
TELL THEM WHAT?
ABOUT MY NEW QUEEN! THE WOMAN WHO SAVED ME!

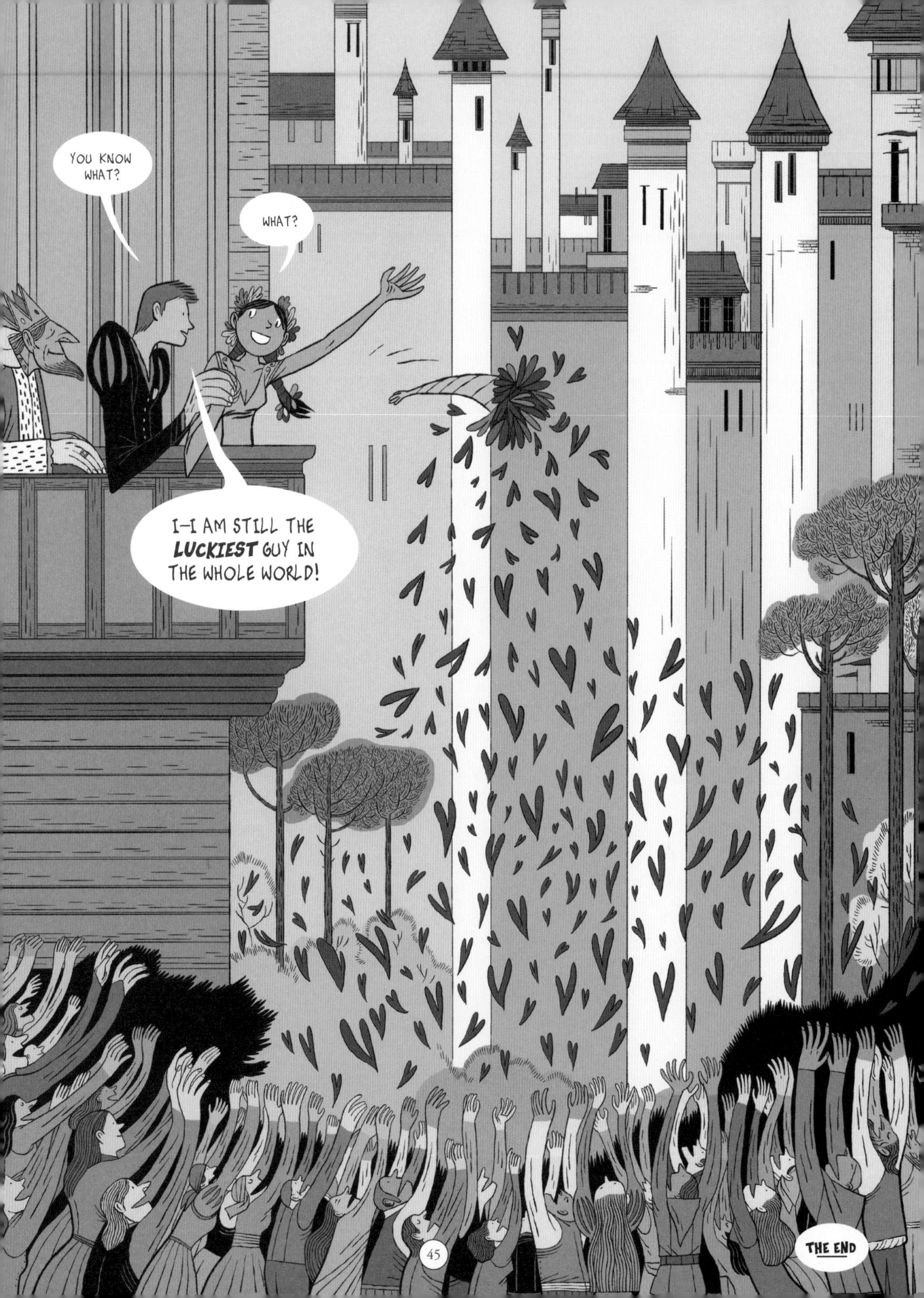
YOU KNOW WHAT?
WHAT?
I—I AM STILL THE **LUCKIEST** GUY IN THE WHOLE WORLD!
THE END

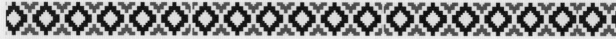

TIME TO SHOW OFF

by Nadja Spiegelman

The fairy tales that endure, that lodge themselves into our minds, are the ones that not only contain the symbols of a culture; they are the ones that speak to our deepest fears and emotions, to the basic foundations of our selves. In *Blancaflor*, a story blossomed about a girl who defies her father, who helps her lover with women's objects — a comb, a mirror, a bar of soap — a young woman who has the power to transform rocks into flour and then bread. Some version of this story, which follows the format of "The Girl as Helper in the Hero's Flight," exists in nearly every culture. It is one of the oldest and most widespread tales in the world. This story traveled from Norway to

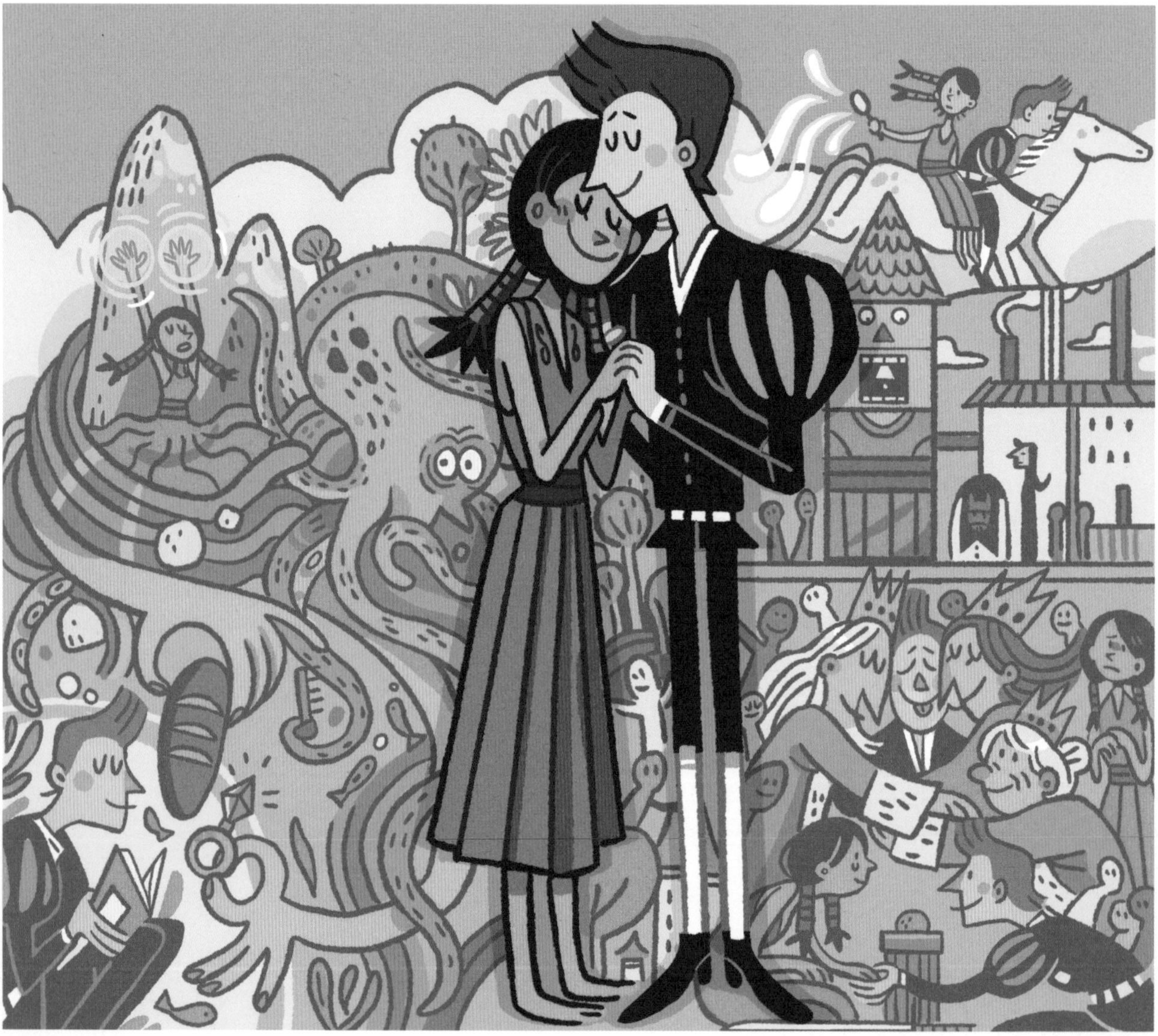

Sergio García Sánchez (who illustrated this tale) and Lola Moral (who colored it) have two children who are also artists: **ALICIA GARCÍA MORAL** *(illustration above)* and **PABLO GARCÍA MORAL** *(illustration on the next page), who contributed here their own visual versions of* Blancaflor. *The family's cat is still working on his.*

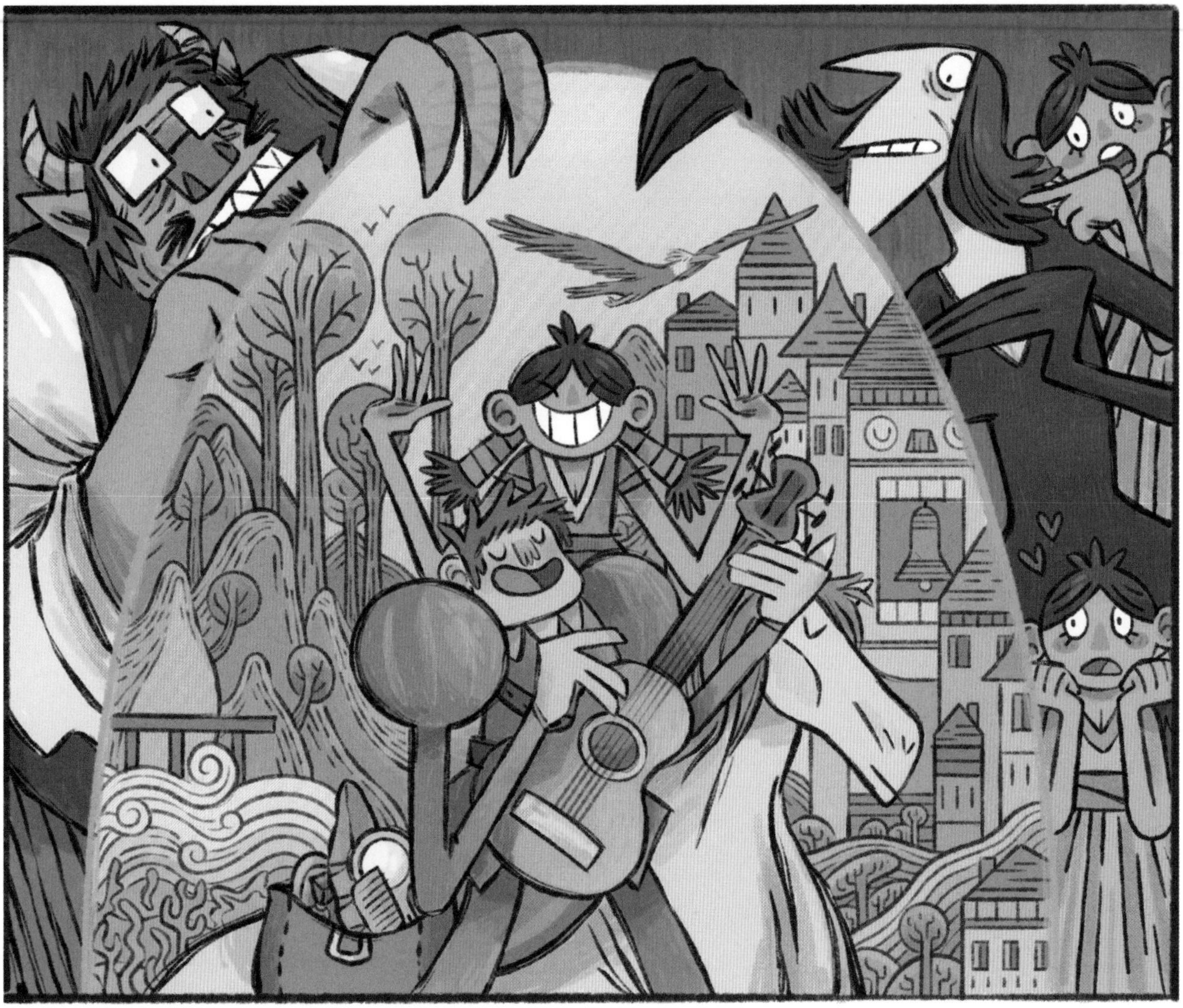

Ireland, from Spain to the Americas. A similar story appears as "The Master Maid" in some cultures, and of course Blancaflor is cousin to Medea, the helper-maiden to Jason in his search for the Golden Fleece. In Latin America, the story of Blancaflor intermingled with Native and Maya tales and became canonical. In some indigenous cultures, the defiance of the ogre was understood as defiance of the landowners and of the Spanish conquerors. The moving of mountains and the flooding of plains echoed the skillful ways in which Indigenous Peoples developed agriculture and brought us so much of the food we eat today: corn and tomatoes and potatoes, beans and squash, among so many others. And yet, while rarely told directly as such, this story, in all its multicultural variants, has always been about the invisible labor of women.

Though much has changed, much has stayed the same, and I was drawn to this tale for its continuing resonance. One still earns far more on Wall Street, trading abstract futures, than as a teacher or a nurse or a mother raising children. Many women know about the sword of pain and the stone of sorrow. Most versions of this tale begin with the prince; my version begins with the girl. In this modern retelling, it is not enough for Blancaflor to discover her powers, to escape the murderous wrath of her parents, to be a helper to the hero. She must also escape from the surrounding patriarchy and learn to take credit for her accomplishments. Of course, women have magical powers. We have all known this since antiquity. Now, it's time for us to show them off.

ABOUT THE AUTHORS

The authors' other collaboration, Lost in NYC: A Subway Adventure, *received six starred reviews and many awards and distinctions, including a School Library Journal's Best Book of the Year and an American Library Association's Notable Children's Book.*

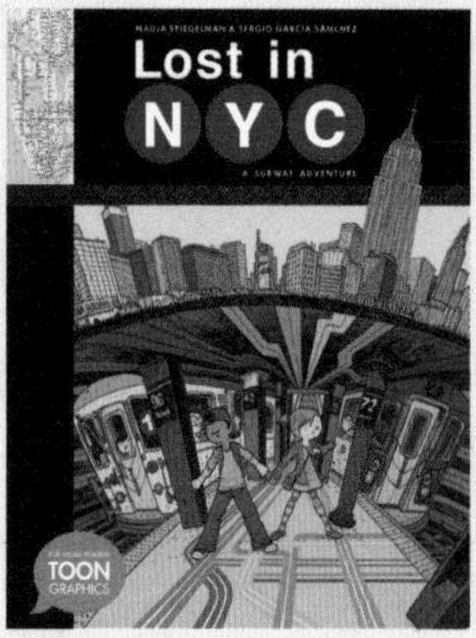
NADJA SPIEGELMAN & SERGIO GARCÍA SÁNCHEZ
Lost in NYC
A SUBWAY ADVENTURE
TOON GRAPHICS

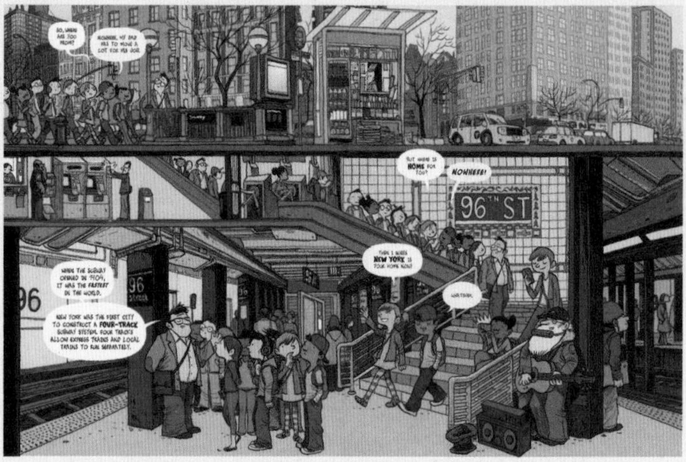
BUT WHERE IS HOME FOR YOU?
NOWHERE!
96TH ST
WHEN THE SUBWAY OPENED IN 1904, IT WAS THE FASTEST IN THE WORLD.
NEW YORK WAS THE FIRST CITY TO CONSTRUCT A FOUR-TRACK SUBWAY SYSTEM. FOUR TRACKS ALLOW EXPRESS TRAINS AND LOCAL TRAINS TO RUN SEPARATELY.
THEN I GUESS NEW YORK IS YOUR HOME NOW!

NADJA SPIEGELMAN is the Eisner Award-nominated author of the Zig and Wikki series of science comics for young children and the editor-in-chief of an international literary magazine. Her memoir *I'm Supposed to Protect You From All This* was published by Riverhead. She is a contributing editor at *The Paris Review* and the co-editor of the 2016-2017 project *Resist!*, a magazine of women's political comics and graphics.

SERGIO GARCÍA SÁNCHEZ, a professor of comics in Angoulême, France, and at the University of Granada, Spain, is one of Europe's most celebrated experimental cartoonists. His work has been published in over forty-five books and translated into nine languages. He lives in Granada with his wife and collaborator, **LOLA MORAL**, who colored the art for this book.

BIBLIOGRAPHY

The Dragon Slayer: Folktales from Latin America, Jaime Hernandez, TOON Books, 2017. *By the co-creator of the comic book series,* Love and Rockets. *Ages 8+*

Tales Our Abuelitas Told: A Hispanic Folktale Collection, F. Isabel Campoy and Alma Flor Ada (Authors), Atheneum Books for Young Readers, 2006. *Twelve stories from varied roots of Hispanic culture. Ages 5-10*

Latin American Folktales: Stories from the Hispanic and Indian Tradition, John Bierhorst, Pantheon Books, 2002. *A collection of Latin American stories sourced from twenty countries.*

The Monkey's Haircut and Other Stories Told by the Maya, John Bierhorst and Robert Andrew Parker (Illustrator), William Morrow and Company, 1986. *A collection of twenty-two traditional Maya tales.*

Fiesta Femenina: Celebrating Women in Mexican Folktales, Mary-Joan Gerson, Barefoot Books, 2001. *Eight stories of extraordinary women in Mexican folklore. Ages 8+*

Mexican-American Folklore, John O. West, August House, 2005. *A range of traditional Mexican-American proverbs, riddles, stories and folk songs.*

The Day It Snowed Tortillas / El Día Que Nevaron Tortillas: Folktales told in Spanish and English, Joe Hayes & Antonio Castro Lopez, Cinco Puntos Press, 2003. *A collection of New Mexican magical folktales for a modern audience. Ages 10-12*

Horse Hooves and Chicken Feet: Mexican Folktales, Neil Philip (Compiler) & Jacqueline Mair (Illustrator), Clarion Books, 2003. *Fifteen classic Mexican folktales. Ages 5-8*

Online Resources:

WWW.AMERICANFOLKLORE.NET *Retellings of folktales, myths, legends, fairy tales, superstitions, weather lore, and ghost stories from all over the Americas.*

WWW.SURLALUNEFAIRYTALES.COM SurLaLune *offers over 40 eBooks, including fairy tale and folklore anthologies, critical texts, poetry, and fiction.*

WWW.STORIESTOGROWBY.ORG *Folk & fairy tales from around the world.*

WWW.PITT.EDU/~DASH/FOLKTEXTS.HTML *Offers a variety of folklore and mythology texts, arranged in groups of closely related stories.*

HTTP://ONLINEBOOKS.LIBRARY.UPENN.EDU/ *An index of over two million books readable for free. (Search for subject: tales.)*